RICHARD ADAMS

Tales from Watership Down

Richard Adams is the author of many bestselling novels, including *Watership Down* (1974), *Shardik* (1976), *The Plague Dogs* (1978), *The Girl in a Swing* (1980), *Maia* (1985), and *Traveller* (1988), as well as several works of nonfiction, including his autobiography, *The Day Gone By* (1991). The winner of the Carnegie Medal and the Guardian Award for Children's Literature, he currently lives in Hampshire, England.

ALSO BY RICHARD ADAMS

Watership Down
Shardik
The Plague Dogs
The Girl in a Swing
The Unbroken Web
Maia
Traveller

TRAVEL

Voyage Through the Antarctic
(with R. M. Lockley)

PICTURE BOOKS IN VERSE

The Tyger Voyage
The Ship's Cat

NATURE

A Nature Diary
Nature Through the Seasons
(with Max Hooper)
Nature Day and Night
(with Max Hooper)

AUTOBIOGRAPHY

The Day Gone By

Tales from
Watership Down

Tales from Watership Down

RICHARD ADAMS

With Decorations by John Lawrence

VINTAGE BOOKS
A Division of Random House, Inc.
New York

FIRST VINTAGE BOOKS EDITION, DECEMBER 2012

The author and publishers wish to thank the following
for permission to reproduce excerpts in the chapter epigraphs:
A. P. Watt Ltd.: Excerpt from "The Municipal Gallery Revisited" by W. B. Yeats.
Reprinted by permission of A. P. Watt Ltd. on behalf of Anne Yeats.
The Continuum Publishing Group: Excerpt from *Auto-da-Fe* by Elias Canetti,
copyright © 1947, copyright renewed 1974 by Elias Canetti. Reprinted by
permission of The Continuum Publishing Group.
Dufour Editions Inc.: Excerpt from "Autumn 1942" from
Collected Poems of Roy Fuller by Roy Fuller. Reprinted by permission
of Dufour Editions Inc., Chester Springs, Pennsylvania.
Frederick Warne & Co.: Excerpt from "The Tale of Mr. Tod"
by Beatrix Potter, copyright © 1912 by Frederick Warne & Co. Reprinted
by permission of Frederick Warne & Co.
Houghton Mifflin Harcourt Publishing Company: Excerpt from
The Affluent Society by John Kenneth Galbraith, copyright © 1958, 1969, 1976, 1984
by John Kenneth Galbraith. All rights reserved. Reprinted by permission
of Houghton Mifflin Harcourt Publishing Company.

The Library of Congress has cataloged the Knopf edition as follows:
Adams, Richard.
Tales from Watership Down / Richard Adams.
p. cm.
1. Rabbits—Fiction. I. Title.
PR6051.D345T3 1996
823'.914—dc20
96-17047

Vintage ISBN: 978-0-307-95019-2

Book design by Dorothy Schmiderer Baker
Cover design by Mark Abrams
Cover Painting: Rabbits on a Log *by Arthur Fitzwilliam*
Tait © The Metropolitan Museum of Art. Image Source: Art Resource, NY

www.vintagebooks.com

Printed in the United States of America
10 9 8 7 6 5 4 3 2 1

To Elizabeth, with love and gratitude

Contents

Contents

II

―――――

III

―――――

I am most grateful to my secretary, Mrs. Elizabeth Aydon, who not only typed the manuscript of the book with accuracy and patience but also was of great value in picking up inconsistencies and in offering valuable suggestions during our discussions.

Introduction

The tales in this book have been divided into three parts. First come five traditional stories, which all rabbits know, about the hero El-ahrairah ("The Prince with a Thousand Enemies") and some of his deeds and adventures. Two of these, "The Fox in the Water" and "The Hole in the Sky," are glancingly mentioned by Dandelion and Hawkbit toward the end of Chapter 30 of *Watership Down*, and Bigwig, during his fight with General Woundwort (Chapter 47), hears behind him Bluebell telling "The Fox in the Water" to the does. At the end of Part I have been included two tales, "The Rabbit's Ghost Story" and "Speedwell's Story." The latter seemed worth including as representative of the kind of nonsense tales which rabbits enjoy.

Part II contains four of the many stories which are told of the adventures of El-ahrairah and his stalwart, Rabscuttle, in the course of their long journey home from their terrible encounter with the Black Rabbit of Inlé.

In Part III are further tales of Hazel and his rabbits, which took place during the winter, spring and early summer following the defeat of General Woundwort.

Note on Pronunciation

So many people have asked about the correct pronunciation of "El-ahrairah" that it seemed to be worth including a short note.

The first two syllables are pronounced "Ella" (like the girl's name). These are followed by the single syllable "hrair," rhyming with "fair," and finally "rah," rhyming with "spa."

All the syllables are equally stressed except the "la" in "Ella," which is almost (but not quite) elided. The two *r*'s should be lightly rolled.

Tales from
Watership Down

PART I

I

The Sense of Smell

. . . noses have they, but they smell not.

PSALM 115

Who dares wins.

MOTTO OF THE SPECIAL AIR SERVICE

"Tell us a story, Dandelion!"

It was a fine May evening of the spring following the defeat of General Woundwort and the Efrafans on Watership Down. Hazel and several of his veterans—those who had been with him ever since leaving Sandleford—were lying on the warm turf, full of grass and comfortably relaxed. Nearby, Kehaar was pecking among the low tussocks, not so much feeding as using up the day's remains of his continual, restless energy.

The rabbits had been chatting together, recalling some of their great adventures of the previous year: how they had left the Sandleford warren after Fiver's warning of imminent disaster; how they had first come to Watership Down and dug their new warren, only to realize that there was not a single doe among them. Hazel had recalled the ill-judged raid on Nuthanger Farm, in which he had nearly lost his life. This had reminded several of them of their journey to the great river, and Bigwig had told yet again of the time he had spent in Efrafa as a supposed officer of General Woundwort; and how he had persuaded Hyzenthlay to form the group of does who had broken out in the thunderstorm. Blackberry had tried but could not explain his trick with the boat, which had enabled them to escape down the river. Bigwig, however, had refused to tell of his underground fight with General Woundwort, insisting that he wanted only to forget it; so instead, Dandelion had recounted how the Nuthanger dog, let loose by Hazel, had pursued him and Blackberry into the midst of the Efrafans gathered on the Down. He had hardly finished, when there arose the well-worn cry: "Tell us a story, Dandelion! Tell us a story!"

Dandelion did not respond immediately, seemingly reflecting as he nibbled the grass and took a few hops to a sunnier patch before settling himself again. At length he replied, "I think I'll tell you a new story this evening; one that you've never heard before. It's about one of the greatest of all the adventures of El-ahrairah."

He paused, sitting up and rubbing his front paws over his nose. No one hurried the master storyteller, who appeared, by taking his time, to be rather relishing his standing among the group. A light breeze stirred the grass, and a lark, ending its song, dropped down near them, paused for a time and then began another ascent.

*

There was a time (said Dandelion), long ago, when rabbits had no sense of smell. They lived as they do now, but to have no sense of smell was a terrible disadvantage. Half the pleasure of a summer morning was lost to them, and they couldn't pick out their food in the grass until they actually bit into it. Worst of all, they couldn't smell their enemies coming, and this meant that many rabbits fell victim to stoats and foxes.

Now, El-ahrairah perceived that although his rabbits had no sense of smell, their enemies and other creatures—even the birds—possessed it, and he determined that he would seek out that extra sense and win it for his people, whatever the cost. He began to seek advice everywhere he could, asking where the sense of smell was to be found. But no one knew, until at last he asked a very old, wise rabbit in his warren, named Heartsease.

"I can recall that when I was young," said Heartsease, "our warren gave shelter to a wounded swallow—one who had traveled far and wide. He pitied us because we had no sense of smell, and he told us that the way to the sense of smell lies through a land of perpetual darkness, where it is guarded, he said, by a band of fierce and dangerous creatures known as the Ilips, who live in a cave. More than this he did not know."

El-ahrairah thanked Heartsease and, after deliberating for a long time, went to see Prince Rainbow. He told him that he meant to go to that land and asked him for his advice.

"You had much better not attempt it, El-ahrairah," said

Prince Rainbow. "How do you think you are going to find your way through a land of perpetual darkness to a place you don't know? Even I have never been there, and what's more, I don't intend ever to do so. You'll only be throwing your life away."

"It's for my people," replied El-ahrairah. "I'm not prepared to see them hunted down day after day for want of a sense of smell. Is there no advice you can give me?"

"Only this," said Prince Rainbow. "Don't tell anyone that you meet on your journey why you are going. There are some very strange creatures in that country, and if it were to become known that you have no sense of smell, it might well be the worse for you. Invent some purpose. Wait—I'll give you this astral collar to wear round your neck. It was a gift to me from Lord Frith. It may just possibly help you."

El-ahrairah thanked Prince Rainbow, and next day he set out. When at length he came to the border of the land of perpetual darkness, he found that it began with twilight, which deepened until all around was dark. He could not tell which way to go, and what was worse, he could form no sense of direction, so that for all he knew, he might be going in circles. He could hear other creatures moving in the dark around him, and as far as he could tell, they seemed to know what they were doing. But were they friendly, and would it be safe to talk to any of them? At last, in sheer desperation, he sat down in the dark and waited in silence until he heard some creature moving nearby. Then he said, "I'm lost and confused. Can you help me?"

He heard the creature stop, and after a few moments it replied in a strange but just understandable tongue. "Why are you lost? Where have you come from and where do you want to go?"

"I've come from a land where they have daylight," answered El-ahrairah, "and I'm lost because I can't see and I'm not used to this darkness."

"But can't you smell your way? We all can."

El-ahrairah was about to answer that he had no sense of smell, but then he remembered Prince Rainbow's warning. So he said, "I'm afraid the smells are all different here. They only confuse me."

"So you've no idea what sort of creature I am, for instance?"

"Not the least. But you don't seem fierce, that's one blessing."

El-ahrairah heard the creature sit down. After a little, it said, "I'm a glanbrin. Are there any where you come from?"

"No. I'm afraid I've never heard of a glanbrin. I'm a rabbit."

"*I've* never heard of a rabbit. Let me sniff you over."

El-ahrairah kept as still as he could while the creature, which was furry and seemed to be about the same size as himself, sniffed him over carefully from head to foot. At last it said, "Well, you seem to be very much the same sort of animal as I am. You're not a beast of prey and you obviously have a very strong sense of hearing. What do you eat?"

"Grass."

"There isn't any here. Grass won't grow in the dark. We eat roots. But I think you and I are very much alike. Don't you want to have a sniff too?"

El-ahrairah pretended to sniff all over the glanbrin. In doing so, he found that it had no eyes; that is, what might have been its eyes were hard, small and sunken, almost lost in its head. But for all that, he thought, "Well, if this isn't some sort of rabbit, then I'm a badger." He said, "I don't believe there's anything much to choose between us, except that I . . ." He was about to say "can't smell" but checked himself and finished: "that I'm utterly confused and lost in this darkness."

"But if your right place is in the lighted country, why have you come here?"

"I want to talk to the Ilips."

He could hear the glanbrin startle and jump. "Did you say 'the Ilips'?"

"Yes."

"But nobody ever goes anywhere near the Ilips. They'll kill you."

"Why should they?"

"Well, they're flesh eaters, for a start, and they're very fierce. But even apart from that, they're the most feared creatures in all this country. They possess evil magic and ugly spells. Why do you want to talk to them? You might as well go and jump in the Black River while you're about it."

Then, since he could see no help for it, El-ahrairah told the glanbrin why he had come to the Dark Country and what he meant to try to do for his people. It heard him out in silence. Then it said, "Well, you're brave and good-hearted. I'll give you that. But what you want to do is impossible. You'd much better go home now."

"Can you guide me to the Ilips?" said El-ahrairah. "I'm still determined to go."

After a long argument, the glanbrin at last gave in and undertook to guide El-ahrairah as near to the Ilips as he himself dared to go. It was all of two days' journey, he said, through strange country where he had never been.

"Then how will you know the way?" asked El-ahrairah.

"Why, by the smell, of course. The whole country's soaked in the smell of the Ilips. Do you mean to say you can't smell it at all?"

"No," said El-ahrairah. "I can't."

"Well, now I *know* you've got no sense of smell. I should stay like that, if I were you. At least you don't have to smell the Ilips."

They set out together. On the way, the glanbrin told a great deal about the customs and way of life of his people, which, it seemed to El-ahrairah, did not differ much from those of his own rabbits.

"You seem to live much the same as we do," he said. "All together in groups, I mean. How was it that you were alone when you met me?"

"It's sad, is that," replied the glanbrin. "I'd chosen a mate, a beautiful doe. Her name's Flairgold. She's much admired by everyone. We were going to dig a burrow and raise a litter. But then along came a stranger, a hulking great glanbrin calling himself Shindyke. He said he meant to fight me and take Flairgold for himself. We fought, and he won. I just wandered away. I felt heartbroken; I still do. It's spoiled my life, really. I don't know what to do with myself. When you and I met, I was just straying. That's why I'm guiding you now. I might as well do that as anything else."

El-ahrairah told him how sorry he was. "It's an all too familiar story," he said. "It's the same where I come from. It's happening all the time. You're not the only one, if that's any comfort to you."

The glanbrin had said "two days," but in that terrible country El-ahrairah could not count days. Also, he kept stumbling and hurting himself because he could neither smell nor see. He became covered in cuts and bruises. The glanbrin was sympathetic and patient, but El-ahrairah could tell that he wished they could get on faster. He was plainly nervous and wanted to get their journey done as soon as possible.

After they had gone a long way, for what seemed to El-ahrairah to be many days, the glanbrin stopped at a place where piles of stones lay scattered all about. These at least El-ahrairah could feel.

"This is as near as I dare go," said the glanbrin. "You must find your own way from here. Use the wind for direction. It stays fairly steady as a rule."

"What do you mean to do now?" asked El-ahrairah.

"I'll wait here for two days, in case you come back, though I know you won't."

"Yes, I shall," said El-ahrairah. "I'll find these stones again, dark or no dark. So I'll only say goodbye for the present, friend glanbrin."

He set off once more into the dark, being careful to go steadily into the light wind. But it was very difficult to keep direction, and he went slowly. The truth was that the darkness was becoming more than he could endure. He was worn out by it and, in spite of what he had said to the glanbrin, was beginning to wonder whether he would be able to bear it long enough to get home. Without the use of his eyes, he was continually startled by every least sound, and was always tripping and falling. This was bad enough, but the silence was worse. He felt that the darkness itself was alive and hated him; and it never changed, never slept, never spoke. All it had to do was to wait for him to go mad, to break down, to give up and surrender. Then he would have lost and the implacable darkness would have won.

Adding to his fear and uncertainty were his hunger and thirst. He had had no grass since he first came into this dreadful country. True, he had not starved, for the glanbrin, explaining that his people lived principally on what he called "brirs," a kind of wild carrot, had smelled some out and dug them up. They were succulent and quenched thirst as well as hunger. But without the glanbrin he would never be able to find any more. He prayed to Frith for courage, though he could not help doubting whether even Lord Frith was stronger than this darkness.

Yet still he went on, as steadily as he could, for he knew that if he did not, it would be the end of him. He felt desperately lonely and would have given anything to have Rabscuttle beside him. Rabscuttle had begged to come, but El-ahrairah had firmly refused him.

Hours passed. At least the wind was steady, but he had no idea how far he had still to go or how long it would take. It would be as bad now to go back as to go on, he thought.

Just as this depressing notion was passing through his mind, he heard in the dark the movement of some creature coming toward him. He could tell that it was big—far bigger than himself—and that it felt entirely confident and secure. He froze stock-still, hardly daring to breathe and hoping that the creature, whatever it was, might pass him by.

However, it did nothing of the kind. It must have smelled him out even before he had become aware of it. It came straight up to him, paused a few moments and then pinned him down under one enormous, soft paw. He could feel the retracted claws. Then it spoke—and he could more or less understand it—to another creature close by.

"I've got it here, Zhuron, whatever it is."

He heard the approach of other creatures like itself. In a few moments he was surrounded by them, all sniffing and touching him with their great paws.

"It's some kind of glanbrin," said one of them.

"What are you doing here?" said another. "Answer. Why have you come?"

"Sir," replied El-ahrairah, scarcely able to speak for terror, "I have come from the country of the sun, and I am looking for the Ilips."

"We are the Ilips. We kill all strangers. Did no one tell you that?"

Just at this moment, another of the Ilips spoke.

"Wait. It's wearing some sort of collar."

Another of the Ilips put its muzzle down to his neck and sniffed at the collar which Prince Rainbow had given him.

"This is an astral collar." He felt all the creatures round him draw back a little.

"Where did you get this?" the first Ilip asked him. "Did you steal it?"

"No, sir," replied El-ahrairah. "It was given to me before I set out: a gift from Lord Frith; a token of friendship to keep me safe among your people."

"From Lord Frith, you say?"

"Yes, sir. Prince Rainbow himself put it round my neck."

There was silence, then, for some little while. He was released from under the Ilip's paw, and another of them said, "Well, why have you come and what do you want with us?"

"Sir," answered El-ahrairah, "my people, who are called 'rabbits,' have no sense of smell. This makes their lives miserable and dangerous, and they suffer, as you would suppose. I learned that your people alone have the power to confer this gift, and I have come to beg you to bestow it on my people."

"You are the chief of these creatures, then, these 'rabbits,' are you?"

"Yes, sir."

"And you've come alone?"

"Yes, sir."

"You don't lack courage, do you?"

El-ahrairah said nothing, and again there was silence. They were all round him, and he felt himself choking in their hot breath. At length the same one said, "It is true that for many years we were the guardians of the Sense of Smell. But we had no use for it, because no other creatures seemed to lack it. It became a burden to us, and at last we gave it away."

"To whom?" asked El-ahrairah tremblingly.

"Why, to the King of Yesterday, of course. We couldn't give it to anyone else, could we?"

El-ahrairah felt bitterly mortified. To have accomplished such a journey, and to have been spared by the terrible Ilips, only to learn that they no longer possessed what he was seeking, was grievous indeed. But still he did his best to pull himself together.

"Sir," he said, "where is that King and which way shall I go to find him?"

He heard them conversing together, and at length the

first Ilip said, "It would be too far for you to walk. You would lose your way. You would starve and die. You may come with me. I will take you on my back."

Full of gratitude, El-ahrairah prostrated himself before the Ilips and thanked them again and again. Finally one of them said, "Here you go, then," took him between its teeth and put him down on the first Ilip's back. It was roughly furred, and he had no difficulty in holding on.

They set out, going what seemed very fast. As they went, El-ahrairah explained to the Ilip that his friend the glanbrin was waiting for him at the place of stones, and asked whether they could go by that way.

"We can stop there, certainly," replied the Ilip. "It's on our way. But directly your friend smells me, he'll run."

"If you could put me down, sir, a little way off," said El-ahrairah, "I'll find him and explain. Then you could come up to us and take us both."

To this the Ilip agreed. El-ahrairah found the glanbrin, who at first was terrified at the very thought of riding on an Ilip's back. At length, however, El-ahrairah persuaded him, and the Ilip set out again, carrying them both.

Traveling at the Ilip's speed, it seemed no distance at all to the place where El-ahrairah had first met the glanbrin. When they got there, he told the Ilip the story of his friend's loss of his beautiful doe.

"Is it far to the burrow you left?" asked the Ilip.

"Oh, no, sir," replied the glanbrin. "It's quite close by."

Guided by the glanbrin, the Ilip took them there.

When Shindyke, the great buck who had taken Flairgold for himself, smelled the Ilip outside the burrow, he came out and ran away as fast as he could go. The glanbrin explained everything to Flairgold, who was delighted to take him back as her mate. She said she had hated Shindyke but had been given no choice.

The glanbrin and El-ahrairah said goodbye to each other with much sincerity and mutual gratitude, and the Ilip set out once more with El-ahrairah to the court of the King of Yesterday.

Soon they were in twilight, and never had El-ahrairah been more glad to see it. The Ilip put him down on the edge of the forest.

"The King's court's over there," he said. "I'll leave you now. I'm glad to have been able to help a friend of Lord Frith."

With this the Ilip disappeared into the forest, and El-ahrairah set off toward the court.

As he came out from among the trees, he found himself crossing a rough field, full of weeds. Upon the further side was a straggling hawthorn hedge and an old, half-broken gate. El-ahrairah, slipping through the gate, was confronted by a creature about the same size as himself, with long ears like his own but having a long tail. He greeted him politely and asked where he could find the King of Yesterday.

"I can take you to him," said the creature. "Are you by any chance an English rabbit? Yes? Well, I always thought it was bound to come."

"And you?" asked El-ahrairah.

"I am a potoroo. We'll go this way, down toward the river. The King will probably be in the big courtyard."

They went down the field together and through a gap in the hedge to the bank of a very still river, which appeared to El-ahrairah to be scarcely flowing at all. His companion spoke quietly to a kind of heron, brown-plumaged and with a black head, which was wading in the shallows. The bird took a few steps across to them and stared intently at El-ahrairah, who felt uncomfortable under its scrutiny.

"An English rabbit," said the potoroo. "Just come. I'm taking him to the King."

The heron made no reply but merely resumed its listless wading. El-ahrairah and his companion went on along the bank. The path led into a gloomy shrubbery, planted with yew and laurel, beyond which stood some old sheds, forming three sides of a kind of courtyard. The floor was of earth beaten (or trodden) hard, and here were lying a number of animals, all unknown to El-ahrairah. Among them, in the center, stood a great, horned beast somewhat resembling a gigantic cow, but unkempt and shaggy. As they entered the courtyard this animal raised its heavy, bearded head and then came slowly toward them. El-ahrairah felt frightened and turned to bolt.

"You needn't be afraid," said his companion. "This is the King. He won't hurt you."

El-ahrairah, still trembling, lay flat on the ground as the big animal nuzzled him, sniffing with its warm nostrils until he felt wet all over. At length, in a very deep but not unfriendly voice, it said, "Please stand up and tell me what you are."

"I am an English rabbit, Your Majesty."

"What, are they all gone so soon?"

"I'm sorry, Your Majesty, I don't understand."

"Are your people not extinct?"

"Certainly not, Your Majesty. We're numerous, I'm glad to say. I've made a long and dangerous journey to come before you and beg a great favor for my people."

"But this is the Kingdom of Yesterday. Did you know this when you set out to come here?"

"I have heard the name, Your Majesty, but I don't know its meaning."

"Every creature in my kingdom is extinct. How did you get here if you are not extinct?"

"An Ilip brought me on its back through a forest of darkness. The darkness almost drove me mad."

The King nodded his huge head. "I see; yes. You couldn't have come here in any other way. But—the Ilips didn't kill you? You have magic, then?"

"Well, yes, of a sort, Your Majesty. I have the blessing and protection of Lord Frith, and as you see, I'm wearing an astral collar. May I make so bold as to ask what you are?"

"I am an Oregon Bison. I rule this country, appointed by Lord Frith. When you arrived just now, I was about to take a walk among my people. You may come with me."

They set off from the courtyard into the fields beyond. These were full of hundreds of animals, all different, and birds were flying overhead. To El-ahrairah it seemed a bleak, melancholy place, but naturally he said nothing of this to the King. He stopped to admire a bird with a black-spotted body and bright-red wings, tail and cheeks—a kind of woodpecker, as it seemed—which was at work on a nearby tree trunk. He asked its name.

"It's a Guadalupe Flicker," said the King. "We have only too many woodpeckers here; I wish we had not."

As they went on, more and more animals and birds appeared, many of whom spoke to the King and inquired about El-ahrairah. He saw species of lions and of tigers, and a kind of jaguar which rubbed its head against the King's leg and walked beside them for some time.

"Have you any rabbits?" asked El-ahrairah.

"Not one," replied the King. "Not yet."

At this, El-ahrairah felt deeply gratified and even triumphant, for he recalled Lord Frith's promise to him of long ago, that although he and his people should have a thousand enemies, yet they should never be destroyed. He told the King all about it.

"It is entirely by human beings that every one of my subjects has been destroyed," the King told him, as they stopped to admire and talk to a splendid grizzly bear, whose coat of light-brown fur was tipped with silver. "Some, like my Mexican friend here, the men quite deliberately shot, trapped and poisoned out of existence; but many others vanished because men destroyed their natural habitats and they couldn't adapt themselves to live elsewhere."

They were coming to a forest, whose tall trees, tangled together with creeper, actually shut out a large part of the sky. El-ahrairah felt nervous. He had had quite enough of forests for the time being. But the King, it seemed, was concerned only to watch the birds among the outer precincts. Most splendid they were, finches, honeycreepers, dark-plumaged molokai, macaws and many more, all living at peace and acknowledging their allegiance to the King.

"This forest," said the King, "is vast and grows daily. If you went in, you would soon be lost and never find your way out again. It consists of all the forest destroyed by human beings. Of late years it has grown so fast that Lord Frith has told me that he is thinking of appointing a second king to rule it." He smiled. "A king who might well be a tree himself, El-ahrairah. What would you think of that?"

"I would think that Lord Frith, in his wisdom, is justified in all his ways, Your Majesty."

The King laughed. "A very good reply. Come, we'll stroll back now. There is an assembly at sunset, and you'll be able to ask me the favor you are seeking for your people. I promise to help if I can."

They walked back by way of the river, in which the King showed El-ahrairah several fishes—New Zealand Grayling, Thicktail Chub, Blackfin Cisco and others—all of which had become extinct. Back at the courtyard, they found animals and birds already assembling, and as the sun set, the King announced that he would start the meeting.

He began by introducing El-ahrairah, telling them that he had come to the Court of Yesterday to beg for a favor which would greatly benefit the rabbits of whom he was the Chief. Then he asked El-ahrairah to take his place in the middle of all the creatures present and tell them what he had come to ask for.

El-ahrairah spoke to them about his people, of their strength and speed and cunning, and of how they lacked only one faculty to make them rivals of all other animals— namely, the Sense of Smell. When he had finished speaking, he could tell that all the birds and animals felt themselves on his side and eager to help him.

Then the King spoke. "My good friend," he said, "most brave and worthy rabbit, how gladly would I grant your request. But alas! we in this kingdom are no longer the guardians of the Sense of Smell. It is true that the Ilips gave it to us to keep many years ago, but here, in the Land of Yesterday, we were never able to put it to any use. Then one day an emissary, a gazelle, came to us from the King of Tomorrow, requesting us to lend them the Sense of Smell. They would return it soon, the gazelle promised. So we gave it to him to take back to their King. But you know how it often is with things that are lent: they don't get returned. Having no use for it here, we forgot all about it; and so, I dare say, have they. It must still be at the court of the King of Tomorrow, and I can only advise you, friend rabbit, to seek it there. I am very sorry to disappoint you."

"Is it far?" asked El-ahrairah. He was thinking that if anyone else referred him elsewhere he would explode with frustration; yet what could he do?

"I fear it certainly is far," replied the King. "It must be many days' journey for a rabbit. Dangerous too."

"Your Majesty," cried a brindled, heavy-muzzled gray wolf. "I will carry him there on my back. It will be no distance for me."

El-ahrairah gladly accepted the offer, and that very night they set out together, for the Kenai wolf told him that he preferred traveling by night and sleeping by day.

They traveled for three nights; a long way, but El-ahrairah saw little of the countries through which they passed, because of the all-surrounding darkness. The wolf told him that his people had once been among the largest of all wolves. They had inhabited a place called the Kenai Peninsula, in a bitterly cold country far away, where they had lived by hunting a huge kind of deer called "moose." "But the human beings killed us all," he said.

As dawn was about to break at the end of their third night together, the wolf put El-ahrairah gently down and said, "I can take you no further, friend rabbit. I'm extinct, you see, so I can't go into the Land of Tomorrow. You'll have to ask your way to the King's court from here. Good luck! I hope all goes well and that they give you what you are seeking so bravely."

So El-ahrairah entered the Land of Tomorrow and began asking the way to the King's court. He asked raccoons, chipmunks, groundhogs and many more. All were friendly and helpful, and his journey was easy enough. At length, one morning, he heard in the distance an alarming clamor, as though all the animals in the world were fighting together.

"Whatever is all that noise?" he asked a koala bear perched in a nearby tree.

"That, cobber? Oh, that's only a meeting at the King's court," answered the koala. "Noisy lot, aren't they? You soon get used to it, though. Some are a bit ocker, but they're nearly all quite harmless."

El-ahrairah went on until he came to two great ornamental gates, all of gold, set in a hedge of copper-leaved prunus in white bloom. As he was looking through the gates at the garden beyond, a peacock, its tail fully spread, came up and asked him what he wanted. El-ahrairah replied that he had made a long and dangerous journey to seek an audience of the King.

"I'll let you in with pleasure," said the peacock, "but you'll find it hard to get near the King and talk to him. There are thousands of creatures all trying to do that. The King holds a meeting every day. Today's will be starting quite soon now. You'd better go in and try your luck." And he swung open one of the gates.

Going into the gardens, El-ahrairah found himself pressed among a crowd of animals, birds and reptiles, all chattering together and all determined to speak with the King if they could. He felt dispirited, for he could not imagine how he could possibly manage to get to the King in competition with a throng like this. As well as he could, he made his way through them to the further side.

Here he found a long, grassy field, which sloped smoothly down to a flat lawn at the bottom. A few animals were already gathering together on the slope, and El-ahrairah asked a passing bobcat what was going to happen.

"Why, the King will be coming soon," answered the bobcat, "to hear the requests of animals who petition him."

"Will there be many?" asked El-ahrairah.

"There always are," replied the bobcat. "More than the King can ever hear in one day. Some animals have been coming here for days and still can't get a hearing."

The slope was filling up fast. Looking at all the animals, El-ahrairah felt his heart sink. He would never, he thought, be able to speak to the King with this lot all contending. Never, that was, unless he could think of a clever trick of some kind. He racked his brains. A trick, a rabbit trick! Lord Frith, a rabbit trick!

Suddenly he noticed, not far away at the top of the slope, an ornamental basin, oval and about twice as long as himself, raised upon a stone plinth a little above the level of the surrounding grass. He went up to it. It was full, not with water but with some sort of silver, shining fluid of a kind he had never seen before. It was not transparent, like water. In fact, he could not see through it at all, for the smooth surface, like a mirror, reflected the sunshine overhead and the passing animals.

"What's this for?" he asked another nearby creature, who also seemed to be some kind of cat.

"It's not *for* anything," replied the animal rather crushingly. "It's called quicksilver. It was given to the King some time ago as a present, and he had it put here so that everyone can admire it."

Then El-ahrairah moved like lightning. He put his front paws on the edge of the basin, pulled himself up and leaped into the pool. The quicksilver did not behave like water. It was thicker and more buoyant. Try as he would, he could not get beneath the surface. He rolled about, struggling. There were a lot of animals now, all round the edge of the pool. "Who's he?" "What's he think he's doing?" "Get him out. He's got no business to . . ." "Oh, it's one of those stupid rabbits." "Come out, you!"

El-ahrairah clambered out with difficulty. He was not soaked with the stuff, but it had gone down among his fur and broken up into little droplets all over him. He shed them as he moved. Some of the animals were trying to hold him back, but he struggled free, turned, dashed to the foot of the slope and sat down at the front of the crowd just as the King, with three or four companions, came in from one side and stood looking up at his subjects.

He was a magnificent stag. His smooth coat shone in the sunlight like that of a groomed horse. His black hooves also shone, and he carried his superb, branching antlers with such grandeur and majesty that he instantly silenced the whole, chattering assembly. Walking to the center of the lawn, he turned to let his kindly gaze travel slowly here and there among his subjects.

When he noticed El-ahrairah, glittering silver not more than thirty feet away, he stared at him intently.

"What sort of animal are you?" he asked in a deep, smooth voice—the voice of one who never hurried and was always obeyed.

"May it please Your Majesty," replied El-ahrairah, "I'm an English rabbit, come from very far to petition for your royal bounty."

"Come here," said the King.

El-ahrairah came forward and sat up, rabbit fashion, before the King's gleaming front hooves.

"What is it you want?" asked the King.

"I am here to plead for my people, Your Majesty. They have no sense of smell—none at all—and this not only hinders them greatly in feeding and in finding their way about, but also leaves them in great danger from their enemies the predators, whom they can't smell coming. Noble King, only help us, I beg."

Again there was silence. The King turned to one of his retinue. "Have I this power?"

"You have, Your Majesty."

"Have I ever used it?"

"Never, Your Majesty."

The King seemed to be reflecting. Very quietly, he

spoke to himself. "But this would be to assume the power of Lord Frith: to confer upon a whole species a faculty they lack."

Suddenly El-ahrairah cried out loudly to the King, "Your Majesty, do but give us this sense, and I promise you and every creature here that my people shall become to the human race the greatest scourge and tribulation in the world. We will be to them, everywhere, a relentless bane and affliction. We will destroy their greenstuff, burrow under their fences, spoil their crops, harass them by night and day."

At this, cheering broke out among all the creatures in the audience. Someone shouted, "Give it to him, Your Majesty! Let his people become the humans' worst enemy, as the humans are ours."

The babel continued for some little while, until at length the King gazed round for silence. Then he lowered his beautiful head and pressed his muzzle against El-ahrairah. His tremendous antlers seemed to enclose the Rabbit Prince like an invincible palisade. "Be it so," he said. "Take my blessing to your people, and with it the Sense of Smell, to be theirs forever."

On the instant, El-ahrairah himself could smell: the damp grass, the surrounding crowd of animals, the King's warm breath. He felt so much overcome with joy and gratitude that he could hardly find words to thank the King. All the creatures applauded him and wished him well.

A golden eagle carried him home. When it set him down in his own meadow, the first animals he saw were Rabscuttle and several more of his faithful Owsla. "You did it, then—you did it!" they cried, crowding round him. "We can all smell! All of us!"

"Come on, master," said Rabscuttle. "You must be hungry. Can you smell those splendid cabbages in the kitchen garden over there? Come and help us chew them up. I've tunneled under the fence already."

So all of you who've listened to this story, just remember, when next you steal flayrah from men: you're not only stuffing your bellies; you're fulfilling the solemn promise of El-ahrairah to the King of Tomorrow, as all good rabbits should.

2

The Story of the Three Cows

Cows are my passion.

CHARLES DICKENS, *Dombey and Son*

"You're talking nonsense, Fiver," said Bigwig.

They were sitting in the Honeycomb, together with Vilthuril and Hyzenthlay, one wet, chilly afternoon of early summer. "Of course El-ahrairah must get old in time, like all of us; like every other rabbit. Otherwise he wouldn't be real."

"No, he doesn't," replied Fiver. "He always remains the same age."

"Have you ever met him or even seen him?"

"You know I haven't."

"Who were his father and mother?"

"We aren't told. But you know the story tells that in those first days Lord Frith made all the animals and birds, and that to begin with they were all friends; and El-ahrairah, it says, was among the animals in those days. So obviously he doesn't get older—or at least not in the same way that we do."

"And I'm sure that he does; he *must*."

They broke off the argument for the time being, but

that evening, when several more rabbits were assembled in the Honeycomb, Bigwig resumed.

"If he doesn't get older, how can he be a real rabbit?"

"There's a story about that, if I'm not mistaken," replied Fiver. "I can't remember it at the moment. Isn't there a story, Dandelion?"

"You mean about El-ahrairah and the Three Cows?"

"The Three Cows?" said Bigwig. "What on earth have three cows got to do with it? That *must* be wrong."

"Well, I can tell you the story," said Dandelion, "as it was told to me—oh, a long time ago, before we came here. But I can't add anything to it or try to explain it. You'll just have to hear it—all of it—for yourselves, and that's the best I can do."

"Right you are!" said Bigwig. "Let's all hear it. Three cows, indeed!"

They say, you know (began Dandelion), that long ago El-ahrairah lived for a time on these very downs. He lived as we do, as merrily as could be, eating the grass and making occasional expeditions to the grounds of the big house at the bottom to steal flayrah. His happiness would have lasted forever if he had not begun to feel, little by little, a change in himself. He knew well enough what it meant. Gradually, he was growing old. He knew this mainly because his marvelous hearing was becoming less keen and there was a stiffness in one of his front paws.

One morning, as he was feeding in the dew outside his burrow, he saw a yellowhammer bobbing about among the thorn and juniper bushes nearby. At length he realized that this little bird was trying to talk to him: but it was timid and would not do more than flitter from the bushes and back. He waited patiently, and at last—or so it seemed to him—it sang clearly and into his understanding.

> "El-ahrairah would not grow old
> If his mind were strong and his heart were bold."

"Stop, little bird!" said El-ahrairah. "Tell me what you mean and tell me what to do."

But the little bird only sang again:

> "El-ahrairah would not grow old
> If his mind were strong and his heart were bold."

It flew away, and El-ahrairah was left upon the turf to think. He felt bold enough—or so it seemed to him—but where should he look and what was the task that demanded his boldness? Finally he set off to find out.

He asked birds and beetles, frogs and even the yellow-and-brown caterpillars on the ragwort, but none could tell him where he could seek the business of not growing old. At last, after wandering for many days, he met an old, gnarled hare squatting in its form in a patch of long grass. The old hare stared at him in silence, and it took

El-ahrairah some little time to pluck up the courage to ask his question.

"Try the moon," said the old hare, hardly looking at El-ahrairah as he spoke.

Then El-ahrairah felt sure that that old hare knew more than he would say unless he pressed him hard; and he went close up to him and said, "I know you are bigger than I am and can run faster, but I am here to learn what you know, and I will press you with all the means in my power until you tell me. I am no foolish, inquisitive rabbit come to waste your time, but one engaged on this search up to the depths of my heart."

"Then I pity you," replied the old hare, "for you seem to have pledged yourself to seek for what cannot be found and to throw your life away in the search."

"Tell me," said El-ahrairah, "and I will undertake whatever you instruct."

"There is only one way you can attempt," replied the old hare. "The secret you are looking for lies with the Three Cows and with no one else. Have you heard of the Three Cows?"

"No, I haven't," said El-ahrairah. "What have rabbits to do with cows? I have seen cows but never had dealings with them."

"Nor can I tell you where to find them," answered the old hare. "But the Three Cows' secret—or rather, the secret they guard—is the only one which can reward your search."

And with this the old hare went to sleep.

El-ahrairah went asking everywhere for the Three Cows, but received no replies, except bantering and mocking ones, until he began to feel that he was doing nothing but make a fool of himself. Sometimes he was maliciously misdirected and went on journeys only to find at the end that he had been tricked. Yet he would not give up.

One evening of early May, when he was lying under a bush of flowering blackthorn and the sun was setting in a silver sky, he once again heard, close by, his friend the yellowhammer singing among the low-growing branches.

"Come here, friend," he called. "Come and help me!"

Then the yellowhammer sang:

> "El-ahrairah, behind and before
> The bluebell wood and the wide downs o'er,
> El-ahrairah need search no more."

"Oh, where? Where, little bird?" cried El-ahrairah, springing up. "Only tell me!"

> "Now by my wings, my tail and beak,
> The First Cow isn't far to seek.
> Just under the Down, in the neighborhood,
> Lies the brindled cow's enchanted wood."

The yellowhammer flew away and left El-ahrairah sniffing among the first burnets and early purple orchids. He was puzzled, for he knew that there was no wood anywhere in the neighborhood of the Down. At last, however, he went to the very foot, and there, to his astonishment, he saw a deep wood on the far side of the meadow. In front of the outskirts sat the biggest brown-and-white cow he had ever seen.

This could only be the cow he had been looking for; and El-ahrairah knew that the wood must in some way or other be enchanted, for how else could it have come to be standing where to his knowledge no wood had been before? If he hoped to find what he was looking for, into that wood he would have to go.

He approached the cow cautiously, for he had no idea whether she would attack him, although he thought that if the worst came to the worst he could always run away. The cow simply stared at him out of her great brown eyes and said nothing.

"Frith bless you, mother!" said El-ahrairah. "I am looking for a way through the wood."

The cow said nothing for so long that El-ahrairah wondered whether she had heard him. At last she replied, "There is no way through."

"Yet through I must go," said El-ahrairah.

He could see now that the edge of the wood was thick with thorns and briers, tangled and twisted so that nothing bigger than a beetle could possibly get through. Only where the cow sat was there a gap, which she filled entirely. Perhaps, he thought, she would be bound to move, yet it would be useless to ask her to do so, for had she not said there was no way?

Night fell, and the cow had not moved. In the morning she was still there in the same place, and El-ahrairah knew then that it must be a cow of sorcery, for it seemed to feel no need to graze or to drink. He perceived that he would have to resort to a trick. He got up, still watched by the cow, and wandered slowly away down the length of the outskirts until at last he came to a place where the mass of trees and brambles curved inward. He had hoped for a corner of the wood, where he might try to go round it, but as far as he could see, there was none. He made his way some distance into the curve, came out running and hurried back to the cow.

"Are you sure that no one goes into your wood, mother?" he asked.

"No one enters the wood," answered the cow. "It is sacred to Lord Frith and enchanted by sunlight and moonlight."

"Well, I don't know about sunlight and moonlight," said El-ahrairah. "But round that curving bit, there are two badgers who evidently mean to get in. They're digging like fury, and it won't take them long."

"They have no chance," replied the cow. "The enchantment is too strong. Nevertheless, I had better go and stop them." She clambered up and went lumbering away.

As soon as she had rounded the corner by the curve, El-ahrairah lost not a moment, but dashed through the open gap and found himself in the strange light of the wood.

It was not like any wood he had ever known. To start

with, it was full of odd sounds: frightening sounds, which might have come from the trees or might have been made by animals; though what animals he could not tell. Furthermore, he could not find a single track or path. Sometimes he thought he could smell and hear water, but when he tried to go toward it he became confused. To go through the wood was something he had supposed would be easy to a rabbit of his knowledge and experience, but soon he found it was otherwise and that he was wandering in circles. He also felt sure that despite the noises, there was not a bird or any other living creature throughout the length and breadth he covered.

For four days and more—for hrair days—El-ahrairah wandered starving in that terrible wood, for there was no grass there. More than once he would have gone back, but he no more knew the way back than the way on. At last, one day, he came to a steep slope in the solitude, and at the foot of the slope ran a little stream, all overgrown. He determined to follow that stream, for sooner or later it must, he felt sure, run out of the wood, though on which side he could not tell.

He followed the stream for two days and became so faint that he could go no further. He sank down and fell asleep, and when he woke could see that lower down the course of the stream there was a faint glow of brighter light. He stumbled toward it and at last came to a marshy place, where the water ran out of the wood into a smooth, green meadow stretching away as far as he could see. The grass was the best he had ever eaten and full of cowslips. He ate all he wanted, found a hole in a bank and slept for a full day and night.

When he woke he began to wander across the great meadow. It was full of flowers: buttercups and moon daisies, tormentil and orchid and salad burnet. His energy returned, and he began to wonder which way he ought now to take in his strange journey. As he rested on a bank where clumps of scented valerian were growing, he was startled to see once again his friend the yellowhammer, flitting about in the hedge.

> "El-ahrairah! El-ahrairah!" [sang the yellowhammer]
> "El-ahrairah is healed and full,
>   And he must seek the great white bull."

El-ahrairah was puzzled at this, for he had supposed that he would now have to seek the Second Cow, of whom there was no sign. But he trusted the yellowhammer and went on with his journey over the grassy plain. He met no other animals and felt so safe that for two nights he lay down to sleep in the open.

On the third day he came to a place where the grass was all grazed short and trodden, and there, ahead of him, he saw the white bull. He had never seen so noble a creature. His great eyes were blue as the sky, and his long, curved horns were pure golden in color, while his coat was soft and white as summer clouds.

El-ahrairah greeted the bull as a friend, for he could tell that he would not harm him. They sat together in the grass and talked of nothing—of flowers and sunshine.

"Do you live here alone?" asked El-ahrairah.

"Alas! I am alone," replied the bull. "I long for a mate, and in time gone by Frith promised me her whom they call the Second Cow; but I can never reach her, for she is surrounded by a great expanse of sharp rocks and pointed boulders, which cut my legs and break my hooves. I have lived here many months, but I can find no way to pass that cruel ravine."

"Show me the way," said El-ahrairah. "It may be that a rabbit can get through."

Then the white bull led him a long way over the plain, until at last they came to the edge of the ravine about which he had spoken. It was a mass of stones sharp as gorse and thick as brambles, stretching, as it seemed, for miles.

"No bull can ever cross that," sighed the white bull sorrowfully. "Yet that is the only way to the Second Cow."

"A rabbit may very well be able to go where a bull cannot," replied El-ahrairah. "I will go, friend bull, and bring you back word of what I find."

Then El-ahrairah set off to slip in and out of the pointed boulders and between the sharp rocks. It was hard going even for a rabbit, and many times he was forced to stop and judge how best he could make his way forward. For three days he went on, over stones which cut his feet and rocks which scraped his sides as he squeezed between them. And at sunset on the third day he came out onto a flat place beyond the stones and saw facing him the Second Cow.

She was gaunt and thin, with an air of lonely sorrow which moved him at once to pity her. He greeted her cheerfully, but she barely answered him, only telling him that he was welcome to make the best of the poor grass and to sleep under the nearest bank. In the morning he again spoke to her as a friend and told her of his journey and of the white bull, but she seemed so distracted and wretched that he could not tell whether she had understood him or not.

El-ahrairah stayed several days with the poor, unhappy cow but could not find any way to dispel her gloom. One day, as he was following her over the thin grass, he saw sharp rocks springing out of the ground in her very hoof-steps. He knew then the secret of her enchantment. The bitter land all around—yes, and the harsh, impassable ravine itself—were the reflection of her stony heart.

El-ahrairah set himself to use all his powers to comfort and encourage the Second Cow. He told her of the shallows of streams at sunset, where minnows swim and marsh marigolds grow thick in the little pools. He told her of sorrel and buttercups in the meadows where cows swish their tails in the long afternoons of June and July. He told her of newborn calves leaping and playing on the grass. He told her everything he could think of which could gladden and lighten her spirits.

At first she seemed to take in little of what he had to

say, but as the days went by and the rain fell and the sun shone in that harsh place, gradually her heart seemed to lighten. At last, one night, she told him that if he would guide her she would do her best to cross the ravine. But lo and behold! next morning, when they came to the edge, they saw the sharp rocks crumbling and green grass springing up between them. It was the melting of her own distracted heart.

Cautiously and gently El-ahrairah led the Second Cow into the ravine, which broke up before them as they went on. After a day and a night they climbed slowly up what had become the grassy edge of the further side, all twined now with ground ivy and dotted with blue bugle, and there waiting for them was the white bull.

Now began a happy time, while El-ahrairah remained with his friends on the great plain. He stayed for the whole winter and the following summer, and as it came on to autumn the Second Cow bore a beautiful calf, whom she named Whitethorn.

Whitethorn and El-ahrairah became great friends, and in the evenings El-ahrairah used to tell her stories about his warren and about his adventures in the days before he had set out on his search. One day, as he was telling Whitethorn of the trick he had played on the dog Rowsby Woof, the yellowhammer flew down to the juniper and sang:

> "Summer spent and almost gone,
> El-ahrairah must journey on."

"Ah! Little bird!" said El-ahrairah. "Don't tell me to leave my friends! I'm so happy here."

But the yellowhammer only sang:

> "Winter comes with snow and sleet,
> Winter freezes to his seat.
> Now, before the first frost's here,
> El-ahrairah must persevere."

So El-ahrairah went sadly to his friends and told them that the time had come for him to set out once more, to search for the Third Cow.

"Have a care, El-ahrairah," said the white bull. "Take great care: for by all I ever heard, the Third Cow is like no other. The Third Cow lives at the end of the world and is able to swallow up the world and all that is in it. Why face such frightful danger? Stay here with us and be happy."

El-ahrairah was sorely tempted, but although he thought for a long time, he could only conclude that the yellowhammer had told the truth and the time had indeed come for him to set out to find the Third Cow.

"Then take Whitethorn with you," said the Second Cow. "She will be your comrade and your guardian and keep you company. Only, I beg you, look after her well. She is very dear to us, but there is nothing I would not do for you, my dear rabbit friend."

So the two set out together; and as I was always told,

this was the hardest part of al El-ahrairah's wanderings, for the way lay over great mountains and through thrilling regions of thick-ribbed ice. Winter came on, and often they were starved with hunger and cold. If he could not have pressed up against Whitethorn, El-ahrairah would have frozen to death. Even the little bird was forced to leave them, for the bitter nights were more than he could endure.

It was many months before the end of that winter, but at last Whitethorn and El-ahrairah, thin as weasels, came slowly down out of the lower hills and found themselves in the land of the Third Cow.

Now, the Third Cow is herself the end of the world. In that land there is nothing that is not the Third Cow—horns and hooves and tail and ears. They could have traveled on and on and still have found themselves nowhere but upon the body of the Third Cow, for it fills the world and is the world. For many days they sought the Cow's head, and at last they found it—a great, staring form of eyes and nostrils and a huge mouth that gaped like a cave. And the Cow spoke to them with the voice of a cave.

"What do you want, El-ahrairah? What are you seeking?"

"I am seeking for my youth," answered El-ahrairah.

"I have swallowed it up," replied the Third Cow. "I have swallowed it as I swallow all that is in the world. My name is Time, and no creature escapes me." And with this she yawned and swallowed half the day.

In the silence El-ahrairah turned to Whitethorn, who stood shivering beside him.

"I am going to find my youth."

"Don't go, El-ahrairah," pleaded Whitethorn. "You will be lost: I know it! Stay with me. Let us go back to my kind father and mother and live in the green meadow."

El-ahrairah said no more. As the Third Cow's mouth opened in a vast snore, he plunged forward and disappeared into the red cavern.

No one knows all that befell El-ahrairah in the heart and stomach of the Third Cow, for it has never been told and never will be. There are no words in which to speak of the dark adventures, formless as dreams, which fell upon him, for he was among everything past: all that the Third Cow had ever swallowed over the long years. What dangers did he overcome? What dreadful creatures did he meet and delude? What did he find to eat? We shall never know. He himself became a dream, a wandering fragment of the past. And whether he could even remember who he had once been the story never tells. The Third Cow is beyond and beyond the reach of any rabbit's understanding.

At last, when he was worn out and exhausted with long stumbling in the entrails of the Cow, he came to a slope that led downward into a faint, dim light. And here lay a lake—a lucent lake of golden milk. This place was nothing less than the udder of the Third Cow, whose milk contains all the blessings of the years and the warmth of all the suns that have ever shone. It is the lake of youth.

El-ahrairah stood gazing at that wonderful lake, and as he gazed he grew faint with wonder. His paws slipped, and all of a sudden he fell head over ears into the golden milk.

He struggled and paddled helplessly, for he could not find a way out. Little by little he felt his strength going from him. He was sinking; he was drowning. He gave himself up for lost.

At the very last, he felt himself drawn downward into a smooth tube and thence into a warm, wet mouth. The next moment he lay spluttering and choking in the open air, on a patch of warm grass, and Whitethorn was bending over him. Near them rose the curve of the Cow's udder. Whitethorn had suckled him out by one of the Cow's teats.

A glow of youth and strength filled El-ahrairah. He danced on the grass. He capered on the stones. He sang to Whitethorn without knowing what he was singing. Whitethorn sang with him, and together, still singing, they turned for home.

The way back was short, for now it was summer and they could travel three times as fast, knowing that all the adventure was blessedly over. All I know of El-ahrairah's return is one strange thing. When he came to the place where the First Cow's enchanted wood had stood, it was no longer there. It had vanished from under the Down as mysteriously as it had appeared, and no one has seen it again, from that day to this. All that was to be seen was the yellowhammer on the thorn, who sang:

> "El-ahrairah has found in truth
> His secret of eternal youth."

*

"Well," said Bigwig, "those were certainly no ordinary cows. It was stupid of me to think they might have been, considering they were an adventure of El-ahrairah. What about Whitethorn? Does she stay the same age too?"

"The stories don't tell any more about her," said Dandelion, "but I'm sure El-ahrairah would never forget a friend who'd meant so much to him."

3

The Story of King Fur-Rocious

Think where man's glory most begins and ends
And say my glory was I had such friends.

w. b. yeats, "The Municipal Gallery Revisited"

The rain was falling across Watership Down in long, billowing clouds, drenching the turf and the beech trees of the hanger. Hazel and several other rabbits were sitting snugly underground in the Honeycomb, some grooming themselves, others chatting of sunny days to come. Kehaar had arrived from the south a few days before and was sitting halfway down his run in quiet contentment.

"Who'll tell a story?" asked Bigwig, rolling over on the floor. "Dandelion?"

"Let someone else for a change," answered Dandelion. "Bluebell, tell us that one you told me last year: about El-ahrairah and the war with King Fur-Rocious. They haven't heard it, I know."

"That was the only time El-ahrairah ever went to war," said Bluebell. "The first and the last."

"Did he win?" asked Silver.

"Oh, yes, of course; but it was how he did it that was so clever. If he hadn't, we wouldn't be here."

*

As we all know (Bluebell continued), rabbits never really go to war; and certainly El-ahrairah had no need to, living his happy life on the downs, until one day, as he was basking in the sun, he got a sudden shock. Rabscuttle came tearing over the grass, and it was plain that he was bringing important news.

"Master!" panted Rabscuttle. "There are thousands of rabbits—stranger rabbits—coming. Enough to eat up the whole Down and turn us out of burrow and home. There's only one thing for it. We must run while there's still time."

"I never run," answered El-ahrairah lazily. "I must see these stranger rabbits for myself. Let them come."

In a few moments he saw them, all right, coming up the Down in hordes. El-ahrairah had never seen so many rabbits in his life. They covered all the grass. In the middle was a huge rabbit, as big as a hare, who came up to El-ahrairah and bared his teeth.

"You're El-ahrairah, aren't you?" said the gigantic rabbit. "You'd better get out of here while you can. This is my Down now, and my rabbits are going to live here."

El-ahrairah looked the rabbit over. "Who are you," he asked, "and what's your name?"

"I'm King Fur-Rocious," replied the rabbit, "and I'm not only lord of rabbits but of rats and weasels and stoats as well. You must hand over all your rabbits to me."

El-ahrairah could see that if he tried to fight King Fur-Rocious he would have no hope at all, so he simply turned round and went away, to give himself a chance to think what was best to be done. But he hadn't gone very far when there was a pattering noise, and Rabscuttle came rushing after him.

"Oh, master!" cried Rabscuttle. "That wretched King Fur-Rocious! He's taken your favorite doe, Nur-Rama, and says he means to keep her for himself."

"What?" cried El-ahrairah. "Nur-Rama? I'll take him to pieces, you see if I don't!"

"I can't imagine how," replied Rabscuttle. "His rabbits are all over the Down, and he's even got rats and weasels that he's holding as prisoners. I'm afraid it's a bad lookout for us, El-ahrairah."

At this, El-ahrairah's heart sank, for it was not at all like Rabscuttle to talk like this. He decided that the best thing he could do was to go and petition Prince Rainbow, who had told him a long time ago that he and his people were free to live on the Down and keep it for their own.

He reached Prince Rainbow soon after ni-Frith, and told him his sorry story.

"I cannot help you, El-ahrairah, I am afraid," said Prince Rainbow, when he had heard all he had to say. "You will have to defeat this King Fur-Rocious yourself. There's no other way."

"But how?" asked El-ahrairah. "He has more rabbits than there are daisies on the Down, and in fact I believe they'll soon have eaten all the grass."

"I'll give you a word of advice, El-ahrairah," said Prince Rainbow. "A tyrant is usually hated by many different kinds of people. This Fur-Rocious no doubt has other enemies, not merely rabbits. You will need friends and allies."

On hearing this, El-ahrairah didn't feel much confidence, but he was so angry about his beautiful doe Nur-Rama that he felt ready to do his best to beat King Fur-Rocious to pieces or die in the attempt. So off he set to make his way back to the Down.

Now, as he was marching along, he met a cat lying in the sun. The cat seemed quite harmless for a change, and El-ahrairah was just passing it by when the cat said, "Where are you going, El-ahrairah?"

"I'm going to beat the daylights out of that rotten King Fur-Rocious," said El-ahrairah, "and make him give me back my doe."

"Well, I'll come with you," said the cat. "I've heard of King Fur-Rocious that he often drowns kittens."

"Jump into my ear, then," said El-ahrairah. And the cat jumped into El-ahrairah's ear and went to sleep, while he still went marching along.

A little further on, he met some ants.

"Where are you going, El-ahrairah?" asked the ants.

"I'm going to beat the guts out of that dirty King Fur-Rocious," answered El-ahrairah, "and make him give me back my doe."

"We'll come with you," said the ants. "That King Fur-Rocious isn't fit to live. His rabbits dig up ants' nests for no reason at all."

"Well, then, jump into my ear," said El-ahrairah. "On we go!"

So the ants jumped into El-ahrairah's ear.

After a while, he met a couple of big, black crows.

"Where are you going, El-ahrairah?" asked the crows.

"I'm going to tackle that disgusting King Fur-Rocious," said El-ahrairah, "and make him give me back my doe."

"We'll come with you," said the crows. "We've heard nothing but ill of King Fur-Rocious. He's a bully and a tyrant."

"Well, jump into my ear," said El-ahrairah. "I can do with the likes of you."

Then, further on, El-ahrairah came to a stream.

"Hullo, El-ahrairah!" said the stream. "Where are you going? You do look fierce."

"No fiercer than I feel," said El-ahrairah. "I'm going to knock the blazes out of that stinking King Fur-Rocious and make him give me back my doe Nur-Rama."

"I'll come with you," said the stream. "I've heard of King Fur-Rocious, and I don't like the sound of him at all. He thinks too much of himself."

"Well, jump into my ear," said El-ahrairah. "No, the other one. I'm sure I'll be glad of you."

Soon after this, El-ahrairah got back to the Down, and there was King Fur-Rocious, surrounded by his heavy rabbits and eating El-ahrairah's grass for all he was worth.

"Ah, El-ahrairah!" said King Fur-Rocious, with his mouth full. "I saw you off this morning, didn't I? What brings you here again?"

"You contemptible, stinking rabbit," said El-ahrairah. "Give me back my doe Nur-Rama and get off my Down!"

"Seize this insolent animal!" cried the King. "Seize him, and shut him up for the night with the Rabid Rats! And we shall see what's left of him in the morning!"

So they shut El-ahrairah up with the Rabid Rats.

As soon as it was dark, El-ahrairah sang:

> "Come out, pussy, from my ear.
> There are rats in plenty here.
> Chase them round until they fly.
> Chew their necks until they die."

Out came the pussycat in a moment. The rats ran in all directions, but she was among them in a flash and chewed them up in hundreds until there wasn't one left alive. Then she went back into El-ahrairah's ear, and El-ahrairah went to sleep.

When morning came, King Fur-Rocious said to his rabbits, "Go and fetch the carcass of that insolent El-ahrairah and throw it out on the grass."

But when they went in, they found El-ahrairah sitting among the dead rats, singing. "Where's that loathsome King?" said El-ahrairah. "Tell him to give me back my doe."

"You shan't have her," said the King. "Take him and shut him up with the Wildcat Weasels! Then we shall see what becomes of his insolent demands."

So El-ahrairah was shut up with the Wildcat Weasels.

In the middle of the night, El-ahrairah sang:

"Come out, crows, by one and two,
    Teach those weasels what to do.
    Peck those weasels on the head.
    Peck them till they fall down dead."

Out came the crows from El-ahrairah's ear and pecked the Wildcat Weasels all to pieces. Then they went back into his ear, and El-ahrairah went to sleep.

In the morning, the King said, "Well, those Wildcat Weasels will have finished El-ahrairah good and proper by now. You had better go and chuck out his body."

But the tough rabbits found El-ahrairah dancing all over dead weasels and demanding his beautiful doe.

"I will not tolerate this insolence!" cried King Fur-Rocious. "We'll make sure of that rabbit tonight. Take him and shut him up with the Savage Stoats!"

They shut El-ahrairah up with the Savage Stoats, and in the middle of the night, he sang:

"Ants, ants, come out of my ear.
    All the Savage Stoats are here.
    Sting their tails and sting their heads.
    Turn them into starks and deads!"

Out came the swarm of ants from El-ahrairah's ear. They crawled all over the Savage Stoats; they burrowed into their brains and stung them so fiercely that they all fell down and died.

Next morning, as before, King Fur-Rocious sent for El-ahrairah's body. But El-ahrairah came himself and said, "You sniveling ruin of a grimy King, give me back my doe!"

"I can't think how this wretched El-ahrairah manages all this," thought the King. "I must find out at all costs."

"You're to tie that rabbit up beside my sleeping place tonight," he said to his followers. "Then I'll see what he's up to and put an end to his tricks for good and all."

So that night El-ahrairah was tied up beside King Fur-Rocious's sleeping place. In the middle of the night, he sang:

> "Come out, stream, come out of my ear.
> Flow all round this stinker here.
> Pour yourself upon his head.
> Drown the blighter till he's dead."

Out came the stream, pouring out of El-ahrairah's ear. It flooded the whole place. It flooded the King up to his neck. The King became terrified.

"Take her; take your doe!" he cried. "Go away, El-ahrairah! Only leave me in peace!"

"No, *you* go!" commanded El-ahrairah. "Release my doe. Then take your disgusting followers and leave my Down forever!"

That morning El-ahrairah was reunited with Nur-Rama, and on the Down was left neither hide nor hair of

King Fur-Rocious and his followers. That was the only war that El-ahrairah ever fought, and that is how he won it.

There was a scuffle from up one of the runs, and in a moment Buckthorn came down, his fur glistening with raindrops.

"Hazel-rah, it's cleared up beautifully!" he said. "The rain's stopped, and it's going to be a fine evening."

A few moments later there was no one left in the Honeycomb except for Bluebell, washing his back and recovering his breath after telling his story.

4

The Fox in the Water

Den Brer Fox know dat he bin swop off mighty bad.

JOEL CHANDLER HARRIS, *Uncle Remus*

"Foxes," said Dandelion, moving a little further into the evening sunshine and nibbling a sprig of burnet, "foxes are bad, I've always understood, if they take to living near you. We've never been troubled by a fox while we've been here, thank Frith, and I hope it stays that way."

"But they've got such a strong smell," said Bigwig, "and besides, you can very often catch a glimpse of them, however cunning they are, because of the color."

"I know. But if a fox happens to take up near a warren, that *is* bad, because it's very difficult for the rabbits to be on the alert always, all the time."

They say (Dandelion went on), El-ahrairah and his warren were once troubled by a fox that made an earth near them. Actually, there was a pair of foxes and they raised a litter, and as both were continually hunting for food, the warren had no peace. It wasn't that they actually lost many rabbits—although they did lose some—but the continual tension and fear began to get the warren down. Everyone was looking to El-ahrairah for some answer to the problem, but he seemed as much at a loss as everyone else. He said little or nothing and everyone supposed that he must be turning the matter over in his mind. But the days went by, and nothing changed for the better. The anxiety was beginning to upset the does.

And then, one morning, El-ahrairah was nowhere to be found. He had disappeared. Even Rabscuttle, his captain of Owsla, could not tell where he might have gone. When he didn't return the next day or the next, there were rabbits who said to one another that he must have deserted them and gone to find a new warren. They felt very low about it, especially when later that day the fox killed another rabbit.

El-ahrairah had wandered away almost in a trance. He felt that he needed time and solitude to think; but even more he felt the need to find, to discover, something that would give him an answer to the warren's terrible problem.

He spent two days on the outskirts of a village. Nothing molested him, but his mind grew no clearer. One evening, as he was lying half asleep in a ditch outside a garden, he was startled by rustling and movement nearby. It proved to be no enemy, however, but only Yona the hedgehog, hunting for food. El-ahrairah greeted him as a friend, and they talked for a while.

"It's so hard to find the slugs, El-ahrairah," said the hedgehog. "They seem to be fewer and fewer, especially in the autumn. I don't know where they get to."

"I can tell you," said El-ahrairah. "They are in all the gardens round here, in this village. The gardens are full of vegetables and flowers and all manner of greenstuff, and that is what attracts the slugs. If you want slugs, Yona, go into the gardens of the human beings."

"But they will kill me," said Yona.

"No, they will not," said El-ahrairah. "It has been made clear to me. They will welcome you, because they will know you have come to eat the slugs. They will do everything they can to encourage you to stay. You will find that I'm right."

So Yona went into the gardens of the human beings, and there he thrived, just as El-ahrairah had said. And from that day to this, hedgehogs have frequented human gardens and been welcome.

El-ahrairah wandered on, his mind still heavy with perplexity. He left the village and soon he came to farmland, where all kinds of crops were being grown. Here, on the outskirts, he found rabbits. They were strangers to him, but they knew who he was and asked his advice.

"Look, El-ahrairah," said their Chief Rabbit, "here's a fine field of greenstuff, as fit to eat as ever was. But the farmer knows how clever we are. He's surrounded it with wire and he's buried the wire so deep in the ground that we can't burrow under it. Look how deep our best diggers have gone. But they haven't been able to get under the wire. What's to be done?"

"There's no use in trying further," said El-ahrairah. "You'd simply be wasting your time. Give it up."

Just at that moment, down flew a flock of rooks. The Chief Rook alighted beside El-ahrairah and spoke to him.

"We mean to fly in there and strip the place. What's to stop us?"

"The man is waiting for you," said El-ahrairah. "He is hiding in the bushes with his gun. If you go in there you will be shot."

But the Chief Rook would not listen to El-ahrairah and led his flock over the high wire fence and into the field of greens. At once two guns began firing, and before the flock could get away, four of them had been killed. El-ahrairah advised the rabbits to leave the place altogether alone, and so they did.

They say that after that El-ahrairah wandered far and wide, and everywhere he went he gave the animals and birds good advice and help. He met mice and water rats and even an otter, which did him no harm; yet he seemed no nearer to what he was seeking.

At last, one day, he came to a great expanse of common land, where the black, peaty soil was covered with miles of heather, juniper and silver birch trees. Here, in the boggy places, there were fly-catching plants and marsh pimpernel, and the wheatears darted from place to place, saying nothing to El-ahrairah, for they did not know him. He went on as a stranger and at last, tired out, lay down in a sunny place, without a thought for the possibility that a stray stoat or weasel might happen along.

As he lay dozing, he felt the presence of some creature close by and opened his eyes, to see a snake watching him. He was not afraid of a snake, of course, and he greeted it and waited to hear what it would say.

"Cold!" said the snake at last. "How cold it is!"

It was a warm, sunny day, and El-ahrairah himself felt almost too snug in his fur. Rather gingerly, he put out one paw and touched the snake on its green length. It was indeed cold to the touch. He pondered on this but could think of no explanation.

They lay together on the grass for a long time, until at last El-ahrairah became aware of something which he had not noticed before.

"Your blood is not like ours," he said to the snake. "You have no pulse, have you?"

"What is a pulse?"

"Feel mine," said El-ahrairah.

The snake pressed closer and could feel El-ahrairah's pulse beating.

"That is the reason you are cold," said El-ahrairah. "Your blood is cold. Snake, you need to bask in the sun as much as you can. When you can't, you will feel sleepy. But when you can, it will warm your blood and make you lively. That's the answer to your problem— sunshine."

They lay in the sun for several hours more, until the snake began to feel active and ready to hunt for food.

"You are a good friend, El-ahrairah," said the snake. "I have heard of the many creatures you have helped with your good advice. I will give you a gift. I will give you the hypnotic power of the snake that is in my eyes. But whatever you use it for, use it quickly, for it will not last. Now stare at me!"

El-ahrairah looked steadily into the snake's eyes and felt his willpower dissolve and even his power to move. At length the snake removed its gaze. "That's right," it said. So El-ahrairah got up and bade it farewell.

Now he began his journey back to his home warren. It was a long way, and it was not until the following evening that he found himself approaching the place.

Now, the story tells that across El-ahrairah's way there ran a brook and that the brook was crossed by a little bridge. And here, on the bridge, El-ahrairah paused to wait, for he knew in his heart what would happen.

Presently, out of the woods above him, came the fox. El-ahrairah saw it coming, and his heart misgave him, yet he remained where he was on the bridge until the fox actually lay down beside him, licking its lips.

"A rabbit!" said the fox. "Upon my life, a plump, fresh rabbit. What luck!"

So then El-ahrairah said to the fox, "Fox you may smell, and fox you may be, but I can tell your fortune in the water."

"Ah ha!" said the fox. "Tell my fortune in the water, eh? And what do you see in the water, my friend? Fat rabbits running on the grass, yes, yes?"

"No," said El-ahrairah. "It is not fat rabbits that I see, but swift hounds on the scent and my enemy flying for his life."

And with this he turned and looked the fox full in the eyes. The fox stared back at him, and he knew that it could not avert its gaze. It seemed to shrink and dwindle before him. And as it did so, El-ahrairah seemed to see, as in a dream, great hounds loping down the hill and even faintly to hear them giving tongue.

"Go," whispered El-ahrairah to the fox. "Go, and never return!"

As though bemused, the fox got up, staggered to the edge of the bridge and half leaped, half fell over it into the water below. Watching, El-ahrairah saw it floating downstream. It struggled out on the further bank and slunk away among the bushes.

El-ahrairah, exhausted by the terrible encounter, turned and made his way home to his warren, where all were overjoyed to see him. The fox and its mate disappeared from the neighborhood. They must have told their story, for no other foxes took their place, and the warren had peace; as we do now, Frith be thanked and praised.

5

The Hole in the Sky

Then shall he answer them, saying,
Verily I say unto you, Inasmuch as ye did it not to
one of the least of these, ye did it not to me.

MATTHEW 25:45

Our virtues now are the high and horrible
Ones of a streaming wound which heals in evil.

ROY FULLER, "Autumn 1942"

El-ahrairah, they say, often used to visit this warren and that, staying a few days with the Chief Rabbit and his Owsla, and advising them about any problems they had. Even the oldest and most experienced rabbits respected his advice and were glad to see him. He was not usually in any hurry to talk about himself, but was a most sympathetic listener, always ready to hear of others' difficulties and adventures, and to give praise where it was deserved. I've often found myself hoping that one day he might drop in here, and I think we ought all to keep a wary eye open for him, for they say that often he's not so easy to recognize: and he has good reasons for that, as you shall hear.

They say that there was once a warren called Parda-rail, whose rabbits thought the world of themselves. According to them, there was no one so spruce, no one so daring, no one so fleet of foot, as the rabbits of Parda-rail; and as for newcomers, well, you more or less had to have a personal recommendation from Prince Rainbow to get in there. The Chief Rabbit was called Henthred, and before you could even speak to Henthred-rah you had to be brought up and introduced by one of the Owsla. And as for his doe, Anflellen—oh! she was a dream of delight until you knew her well enough to realize that she lacked practically all the qualities of an honest rabbit and had other rabbits to do everything for her.

Well, one evening two of the Owsla of this precious warren, Hallion and Thyken, were making their way home after a successful raid on a distant kitchen garden, when near the outskirts of Parda-rail they came upon a rabbit, evidently a hlessi, a wanderer, lying on his side under a thorn-bush, breathing hard, and plainly in a bad way. One ear was torn and bloody, both his front paws were just about encased in dried mud, and he'd lost half the fur on his head. As they approached him, he tried to get up, but after two attempts he fell back and lay where he was. They stopped to look at him and to make sure he wasn't from Parda-rail. As they were sniffing him over, he said to Hallion, "Sir, I'm afraid I'm in a bad way. I'm utterly exhausted and I know I can't run. If I stay here like this, I think one or other of the Thousand is bound to get me. Can you give me shelter in your warren for the night?"

"Give *you* shelter?" answered Hallion. "A dirty, disreputable rabbit like you? Why—"

"Oh, it's a *rabbit*, is it?" put in Thyken. "I was wondering what it was."

"You'd better get yourself out of here," went on Hallion. "We don't want the likes of you hanging about near Parda-rail. Someone might think you came from there."

The hlessi, who seemed desperate, implored them to help him to get to their warren, for he thought it was his only chance. But neither of them would do so, saying that a dirty vagabond like him would only bring disgrace on the name of Parda-rail. They left him still pleading and made their way back without giving him another thought.

About two or three days later, El-ahrairah dropped by, as was his wont in the long days of summer. Henthred greeted him with much respect, saying he hoped he would stay with them several days and enjoy the clover, which was just in season. El-ahrairah accepted the invitation and said he would like to meet the Owsla, whom he hadn't seen for quite some time.

They all came proudly before him, with sleek fur and white-flashing tails, and El-ahrairah praised their appearance and told Henthred that they looked a most likely lot. Then he spoke to them, glancing from one to another as he did so.

"You look the most handsome bunch of rabbits," he said, "that anyone could well wish to see; and I'm sure your hearts and spirits are just as good as your appearance. For example," he went on, turning to one of them, a big buck by the name of Frezail, "what would you do if you were coming home one evening and came upon a wounded hlessi who begged you to help him to your warren and give him shelter for the night?"

"I'd certainly help him," replied Frezail, "and let him stay with us for as long as he liked."

"And you?" asked El-ahrairah, turning to the next rabbit.

"The same, sir."

And so they all said.

Then, before their very eyes, El-ahrairah slowly changed and little by little became the pitiful hlessi whom Hallion and Thyken had encountered a few evenings before. He fell on his side and as he did so looked up at Hallion and Thyken. "And how about you?" he said. But they answered nothing at all, only staring at him in consternation.

"You didn't recognize me, then?" inquired El-ahrairah. All the rest of the Owsla gazed from him to Hallion and Thyken, not understanding what he meant but guessing that there must be something disconcerting between El-ahrairah and those two.

"You—you didn't look like yourself," faltered Thyken at last. "We couldn't tell—"

"Couldn't tell that I was a rabbit—is that it?" said El-ahrairah. "Are you sure you know now?"

Then, before he changed back, he made them all come up close and look at him, "to make sure," he said, "that they'd know me another time." Hallion and Thyken were fully expecting that he'd come down hard on them in some way or other, but all he did was to tell Henthred, in everyone's hearing, what had happened that evening when they'd come upon him lying under the thornbush. They all knew in their hearts that they wouldn't have done any better, and they left him without another word; all except Henthred and a gray-furred, ancient-looking rabbit, whom Henthred introduced to El-ahrairah as Themmeron, the oldest rabbit in the warren.

"All *I* want to say, my lord," quavered Themmeron, "is that if *I* had seen you that evening, I would have known that you were not what you seemed, although I can't say whether I could have told that you were our Prince with a Thousand Enemies. But that you were in disguise I would certainly have known."

"How?" asked El-ahrairah, a little put out, for he had been feeling that no one could have looked more the part of a poor old hlessi than he had.

"Because I would have perceived, my lord, that you didn't look like a rabbit who had seen the Hole in the Sky. Nor do you now, for the matter of that."

"The Hole in the Sky?" said El-ahrairah. "And what may that be?"

"It can't be told," replied Themmeron. "It can't be told. I mean no disrespect, my lord—"

"No, no, that doesn't matter," said El-ahrairah. "I just want to know what you mean by the Hole in the Sky. How can there be a hole in the sky?"

But the old rabbit seemed as though he hardly knew he had spoken. He bobbed his head to El-ahrairah, turned and limped slowly away.

"We generally just leave him to himself, my lord," said Henthred. "He's quite harmless, but I sometimes wonder whether he knows night from morning. I'm told he was a dashing gallant of the Owsla in his time."

"But what did he mean by the Hole in the Sky?"

"If you don't know, my lord, I'm sure I don't," replied Henthred, who, truth to tell, had felt rather nettled at having two of his Owsla shown up for a couple of blighters.

El-ahrairah didn't refer to the incident again. He stayed two or three more days and behaved as though nothing unusual had happened, and, when he left, wished the warren good fortune and prosperity, as he was accustomed to do.

He puzzled a lot over what Themmeron had said, and everywhere he went asked other rabbits what they could tell him about the Hole in the Sky. But no one could tell him anything. At last he realized that he was beginning to be thought a little odd on account of this preoccupation, so he gave up inquiring. Privately, however, he wondered more and more. What could old Themmeron have meant? He came to the conclusion that although he was the Rabbit Prince, he must be missing something really splendid and rewarding: some sort of secret thing. Probably a number of those he had asked knew perfectly well but weren't giving anything away. It must be marvelous, the Hole in the Sky. If only he could find it and somehow or other get through it to the other side, there must be the most miraculous things to be found. He wasn't going to feel contented until he had discovered it.

Well, as you all know, El-ahrairah's journeyings take him everywhere, far beyond the range of ordinary rabbits like ourselves, who are happy enough with green fields and elder bloom, or clean bracken and gorse. High hills and deep woods he was quite accustomed to, and could swim across a river as well as any water vole. But of course, with such wanderings as that, he was liable to encounter some curious and unusual creatures, some of whom were distinctly dangerous. And the story tells that one evening, getting on for nightfall, he was going along a narrow path in some lonely hills when he came face-to-face with a creature called a timbleer—one we know nothing of, Frith be thanked, except that they're fierce and aggressive.

"What are you doing here?" asked the timbleer in no friendly tone. "Get back where you belong, you dirty rabbit."

"I'm doing no harm," replied El-ahrairah. "I'm simply going along this path and not bothering you or any other creature."

"You've got no business here," said the timbleer. "Are you going to turn round and go back, or aren't you?"

"I'm not," said El-ahrairah, "and you've got no right to tell me to."

Then the timbleer rushed upon El-ahrairah, and El-ahrairah grappled with the timbleer among the ragwort and nettles, and there was a terrific battle up and down the path. The timbleer was strong and very agile, and it wounded El-ahrairah badly, so that he lost a lot of blood. But El-ahrairah gave as good as he got, and in the end the timbleer was glad enough to break off the fight and go limping away, cursing El-ahrairah as it went.

El-ahrairah felt weak and dizzy. He sank down where he was on the path and tried to rest, but his wounds were hurting so badly that he couldn't find any position in which he could be comfortable. Night came on, and still he tossed and turned in horrible pain. He must have slept at last, for when he next looked about him, it was becoming light and a thrush was singing from a nearby birch tree. He tried to stand but at once fell down. The pain of his wounds was still bad, and since he couldn't walk he was forced to stay where he was on the path. He began to believe that he would die there.

Soon he became delirious, and lay all day without noticing the passage of time. Sometimes he slept, but even in his sleep he was aware of the pain. He fancied Rabscuttle was with him and begged him for help. But Rabscuttle slowly faded and became a hunched juniper bush on the down where El-ahrairah thought he was lying. Then he thought he was Hazel, telling Hyzenthlay to take good care of the warren while he was gone with Campion on a special Wide Patrol. But all these figments either dissolved or else blended with one another, to be glimpsed as elil seen in the tail of his eye. All day he was turning his head this way and that to try to see them clearly. And meanwhile, some rabbit was whispering jokes in his ear, only he could never quite catch what they were about. He was worn out with pain and fear. He heard a rabbit begging for Rabscuttle to come, and after a while realized that it was himself.

He nibbled at the grass where he was lying, but he could not taste it. "It's special grass, master," said Rabscuttle, out of sight behind him. "Special grass to make you better. Go to sleep."

Next morning he saw, quite plainly, a green fox approaching along the path. Again he tried to stand, but just as the fox disappeared his legs gave way, and he fell on his back and lay there, staring stupidly up at the sky.

Then he began to tremble with fear. In the blue curve of the sky he saw a great rent, a cleft which, he perceived, was an open, gaping wound. The two irregular edges were jagged as though it had been made with something blunt, something which had first cut and then ripped and torn. Here and there shreds of flesh, still attached to the edges, stuck out across the wound, obscuring whatever was behind. All that he could see in the suppurating depth of the wound was blood and pus, a glistening, viscous, uneven surface like a marsh. The edges were messy too, fringed all along with blood and yellow matter on which flies were walking. As he stared in horror, the dead body of a rabbit fell out of the wound, but disappeared as it fell.

To El-ahrairah's distraught eyes, the whole gash seemed to be slowly moving, two parted lips descending to close over him and draw him in. Squealing, he fell from the edge of the path, rolling down the slope several times before he lost consciousness.

When he came to himself he was clear in his head and his wounds were less painful. He felt, now, that he could probably get back home, so that his doe, Nur-Rama, and the faithful Rabscuttle could look after him until he was himself again. He went a short distance rather slowly and then lay down in the sun to do his best to clean himself up.

It was while he was thus resting on the hillside that he became aware of Lord Frith speaking to him in his heart.

"El-ahrairah, you should not undertake any more dangerous adventures; at least for the time being. You don't need to impress your people with more great struggles and journeys. You've done enough. They already love and admire you as much as is good for them or for you. Be lazy and enjoy the summer like an honest rabbit. You have already shown yourself equal to anything likely to come your way."

"My lord," replied El-ahrairah, "I have never questioned your ways, dark and mysterious though they often are. But how . . . how can you suffer to exist in your creation that terrible horror, that wound, that horror past bearing?"

"I don't, El-ahrairah. Look up at the sky. It's not there, is it?"

El-ahrairah looked fearfully up. The Hole in the Sky was no longer to be seen.

"Yet to allow it even for a moment, my lord—"

"It was never there, El-ahrairah."

"Never there? But I saw it with my own eyes."

"What you saw, El-ahrairah, came out of your own delirious mind. It wasn't real at all. I had no power to stop it."

"And that old Themmeron, in Parda-rail—"

"He could perceive that you had never seen the Hole in the Sky. Never speak of it again. Rabbits who have seen it, like yourself, don't want to talk about it, and those who haven't only think you're strange."

El-ahrairah took the experience to heart and felt himself the wiser. He never again saw the Hole in the Sky, and he never spoke glibly about it, especially to rabbits who he could perceive had undergone suffering something like his own.

6

The Rabbit's Ghost Story

There ain't from a man to a sheep in these parts uses
Wailin' Well, nor haven't done all the years I've lived here.

M. R. JAMES, "Wailing Well"

Of the five Efrafans who surrendered to Fiver in the
ravaged Honeycomb on the morning of Woundwort's defeat, four came in a short time to be liked well enough by
Hazel and his friends.

Groundsel, indeed, who possessed a skill in patrolling
even greater than Blackavar's, was, despite his passionate
devotion to the General's memory, a valuable addition to
the warren, while young Thistle, freed from Efrafan disci-
pline, soon developed a most attractive warmth and gaiety.

The exception was Coltsfoot. Nobody knew what to
make of Coltsfoot. A dour, silent rabbit, civil enough to
Hazel and Bigwig but inclined to be distinctly brusque in
his dealings with others, he had little enough to say even
to his fellow Efrafans. On silflay he was nearly always to be
seen grazing yards away from anybody else; and certainly
no one would have dreamed of asking *him* to tell a story.

Hazel, when Bigwig complained to him one day about "that pestilential fellow with a face as long as a rook's beak," counseled letting him alone, since that seemed to be what he wanted, and waiting to see how he would go on as he came to feel more at home.

Bluebell, asked to refrain from jokes at Coltsfoot's expense, remarked that he was always mistaking his silent, mournful stare for that of a cow which had got shrunk in the rain.

The first part of the winter following that momentous summer turned out deceptively mild. November was full of sunny days, bringing out the tiny, white flowers of chickweed and shepherd's purse and even, here and there below the Down, breaking the smooth, black knobs of ash buds and disclosing the tiny, dark-red styles along the nut-bush branches.

Kehaar flew in one day, amid great rejoicing, and brought with him a friend, one Lekkri, whose speech (as Silver remarked) set a new record for total incomprehensibility. Kehaar, of course, knew nothing of all that had happened since the morning after the great breakout from Efrafa. He heard the tale from Dandelion one windy, cloud-blown afternoon of flying beech leaves and rippling grass, and at the end remarked to the uncomprehending narrator that the Nuthanger cat was "verser mean dan plenty cormorants"—a view which Lekkri corroborated with a rasping croak that made a young rabbit nearby jump a foot in the air and bolt for his hole.

Often, on fine mornings, the two gulls could be seen from the north slope of the Down, shining white in the thin sunshine as they foraged together over the plowed field below, already green with next year's wheat.

One afternoon toward the end of the month, Blackavar had taken Scabious and young Threar (the son of Fiver) on a training raid to the garden of Ladle Hill House, about a mile away to the west. ("A soft touch," as he called it.) Hazel had felt some anxiety about the youngsters going so far, but had left the decision (which resembled Edward III's *"Que l'enfant gagne ses éperons"* at Crécy) to Bigwig, as captain of Owsla. They were not back by twilight, and Hazel, after watching with Bigwig in the November nightfall until it was almost completely dark, came down into the Honeycomb in some anxiety.

"Don't worry, Hazel-rah," said Bigwig cheerfully. "Likely as not Blackavar's keeping them out all night for the experience."

"But he told you he wouldn't," answered Hazel. "Don't you remember he said—"

Just then there was a scuffling from up Kehaar's run, and after a few moments the three adventurers appeared, muddy and tired, but otherwise, to all appearances, none the worse.

Everyone felt relieved and pleased. Scabious, however, who seemed very much subdued, merely lay down on the floor where he was.

"What kept you?" asked Hazel rather sharply.

Blackavar said nothing. He had the air of a leader who is reluctant to speak ill of his subordinates.

"It was my fault, Hazel-rah," said Scabious, rather jerkily. "I had a—a nasty turn on the Down, coming back. I don't know what to make of it, I'm sure. Blackavar says—"

"Stupid young fellow, he's been listening to too many stories," said Blackavar. "Now look, Scabious, you're home and safe. Why not leave it there?"

"What was it?" persisted Hazel, in a more kindly tone.

"Oh, he thinks he saw the General's ghost out on the Down," said Blackavar impatiently. "I've told him—"

"I *did*," said Scabious. "Blackavar told me to go and look ahead, round some bushes, and I was out there by myself when I saw him. All black round the ears . . . a huge, great . . . just the way they tell you—"

"And *I've* told *you* that was a hare," interrupted Blackavar with some annoyance. "Frith on a cow, I saw it myself! Do you think I don't know what a hare looks like? . . . Couldn't get him to move until I kicked him," he added to Bigwig in an undertone. "Talk about tharn—"

"It *was* a ghost," said Scabious, but with less conviction. "Perhaps it was a ghost hare—"

"I don't know about ghost hares," said Bluebell, "but I tell you, the other night I nearly met a ghost flea. It must have been a ghost, because I woke up bitten like a burnet, and I searched and searched and couldn't find it anywhere. Just think, all white and shining, this fearful phantom flea—"

Hazel had gone over to Scabious and was gently nuzzling his shoulder.

"Look," he said, "that wasn't a ghost—understand? I've never in my life known a rabbit that's seen a ghost."

"You have," said a voice from the other side of the Honeycomb. Everyone looked round in surprise. It was Coltsfoot who had spoken. He was sitting by himself in a recess between two beech roots: together with his customary silence, the position seemed to set him apart and, as it were, to confer upon him a kind of remoteness and authority, so that even Hazel, bent as he was upon reassuring young Scabious, said no more, waiting to hear what would follow.

"You mean *you've* seen a ghost?" asked Dandelion, quick to smell a story. But Coltsfoot, so it seemed, needed no further stimulation, now that he had found his tongue. Like the Ancient Mariner, he knew those who must hear him; and he had a less reluctant audience, for under his dark compulsion the whole Honeycomb fell silent and listened as he went on.

"I don't know whether you all know that I'm not an Efrafan born. I was born at Nutley Copse, the warren the General destroyed. I was in the Owsla there, and I would have fought as hard as the rest, but I happened to be a long way out on silflay when the attack came, and the Efrafans took me prisoner at once. I was put in the Neck Mark, as you can see, and then last summer I was one of those picked for the attack on Watership Down.

"But none of that has to do with what I said to your Chief Rabbit just now." He fell silent.

"Well, what has?" asked Dandelion.

"There was a place across the fields, not very far from Nutley Copse," went on Coltsfoot. "A kind of little, shallow dingle all overgrown with brambles and thorn trees—so we were told—and full of old scrapes and rabbit holes. They were all empty and cold; and no Nutley Copse rabbit would go near that place, not if there were hrair weasels after him.

"All we knew—and the story had been handed down for Frith knows how long—was that something very bad had happened to rabbits there, long ago—something to do with men, or boys—and that the place was haunted and evil. The Owsla believed it, every one of them, so of course the rest of the warren believed it too. As far as we knew, no rabbit had flashed his tail there in living memory, and long before that. Only some said that squealing had been heard late in the evening dusk and on foggy mornings. I can't say, though, that I ever thought about it much. I just did what everyone else did—kept away.

"Now, during my first year, when I was an outskirter at Nutley Copse, I had a very thin time, and so did two or three of my friends. And the long and short of it was that one day we decided we were going to move out and find a better home. There were two other young bucks with me, my friend Stitchwort and a rather timid rabbit named Fescue. And there was a doe too—Mian, I think she was called. We set out about ni-Frith one cold day in April."

Coltsfoot paused, chewed his pellets for a time, as though considering his words, and then continued.

"Everything went wrong with that expedition. Before evening it turned bitterly cold and the rain came down in sheets. We ran into a foraging cat and were lucky to get away. We were completely inexperienced. We had no idea where we meant to go, and before long we lost all sense of direction. We couldn't see the sun, you understand, and when night fell there were no stars either. And then next morning a stoat found us—a big dog stoat.

"I don't know what they do to you—I've never met one since, El-ahrairah be praised—but we all three just sat there helplessly while it killed Mian; she never made a sound. We got away somehow, but Fescue was in an awful state, crying and carrying on, poor little chap. And in the end, some time after ni-Frith on the second day, we decided to go back to the home warren.

"It was easier said than done. I believe now that we wandered in circles for a long time. But anyway, by evening we were as lost as ever and just plodding on in a kind of hopeless way, when all of a sudden I came down a slope and through a bramble bush, and there was a rabbit—a stranger—quite close by. He was at silflay, browsing over the grass, and I could see his hole—several holes, in fact—beyond him, on the other side of the little dell we were in.

"I felt terribly relieved and glad, and I was just going over to speak to him, when all of a sudden something made me stop. And it was as I stopped and looked at him that it came over me where it was that we must have stumbled into.

"The wind—what wind there was—was blowing from him toward us, and as he browsed he stopped and passed hraka. I wasn't very far away, and he gave off no smell whatever—nothing—not the faintest trace. We'd come blundering through the brambles straight in front of him, and he hadn't even looked up or given any sign of having noticed us. And then I saw something which frightens me even now—I can never get it out of my mind. A fly—a big bluebottle—flew down right on his eye. He didn't blink or even shake his head. He went on feeding, and the fly . . . it . . . it disappeared; it vanished. A moment later he'd hopped his own length forward, and I saw it on the grass where his head had been.

"Fescue was beside me, and I heard him give a little, quick moan. And it was when I heard that that I realized there was no other sound in that dell where we were. It was a fine evening with a light breeze, but there wasn't a blackbird singing, not a leaf rustling—nothing. The earth round all the rabbit holes was cold and hard—not a scratch or mark anywhere. I knew then what I was seeing, and all my senses clouded over—sight, smell . . . I felt a sort of surge of faintness pour up through my body. The whole world seemed to topple away and leave me alone in that dreadful place of silence, where there were no smells. We were Nowhere. I caught a glimpse of Stitchwort beside me, and he looked like a rabbit choking in a snare.

"It was then that we saw the boy. He was crawling on

his stomach through the bushes a little to one side of us—downwind of the rabbit on the grass. He was a big boy, and all I can say is that men may have looked like that once, but from what little I've seen of them, they don't anymore. There was a kind of dirty, faraway wildness about him, like the place itself. His clothes were foul and torn. He had old boots too big for him and a stupid, cruel face with bad teeth and great warts on one cheek. And he, too, made no sound and had no smell.

"In one hand he was holding a forked stick with a sort of loop hanging from it, and as I watched he put a stone into it and pulled it back nearly to his eye. Then he let go, and the stone flew out and hit the rabbit on the right hind leg. I heard the bone break, and the rabbit leaped up and screamed. Yes, I heard that, all right—I still hear it, and dream about it too. Can you imagine what a breathless, a lungless scream might be like? It seemed to be in the air rather than to come from the rabbit kicking on the grass. It was as though the whole place had screamed.

"The boy stood up, cackling, and now the hollow seemed to be full of rabbits we couldn't see, all running for those cold, empty holes.

"You could see he was enjoying what he'd done—not just that he'd shot himself a rabbit but that it was hurt and screaming. He went over to it, but he didn't kill it. He stood looking down at it and watching it kick. The grass was bloody, but his boots left no mark, either on the grass or on the mud.

"What was going to happen next I don't know. Thank

Frith I'll never know. I believe my heart would have stopped—I should have died. But suddenly, like a noise coming from a long way outside when you're underground, I heard men's voices approaching and smelled a white stick burning. And I was glad—yes, I was *glad* as a goldfinch on the tall grass—to hear those voices and smell that white stick. A moment later they came pushing through the flowering blackthorn, scattering the white petals all over the ground. There were two of them, big, flesh-smelling men, and they saw the boy—yes, they saw him and called out to him.

"How can I explain to you the difference between those men and the rest of that place? It was only when they came shoving in, rasping on the thorns, that I understood that the rabbit and the boy and—everything there—they were like acorns falling from an oak tree. I saw a hrududu once roll down a slope by itself. Its man had left it on a slope, and I suppose he'd done something wrong—it just went slowly rolling down into the brook below, and there it stopped.

"That's what they were like. They were doing what they had to do—they had no choice—they'd done it all before—they'd done it again and again—there was no light in their eyes—they weren't creatures that could see or feel—"

Coltsfoot stopped, choking. In dead silence Fiver left his place and lay down beside him, between the tree roots, speaking in a very low voice which no one else could hear.

After a long pause, Coltsfoot sat up, shook his ears and went on.

"Those . . . those . . . sights . . . those things . . . the rabbit and the boy—they melted, even as the men spoke. They vanished, like frost on the grass when you breathe on it. And the men—they noticed nothing strange. I believe now that they saw the boy and spoke to him as part of a kind of dream, and that as he and his poor victim vanished, they remembered nothing of it. Well, be that as it may, they'd evidently come there because they'd heard the rabbit squeal, and you could see why at once.

"One of them was carrying the body of a rabbit dead of the White Blindness. I saw its poor eyes and I could see, too, that the body was still warm. I don't know whether you know how men go about this dirty work, but what they do is to put the still-warm body of a dead rabbit down a hole in a warren before the fleas have left the ears. Then, as the body turns cold, the fleas go to other rabbits, who catch the White Blindness from them. There's nothing you can do but run away—and that only if you realize in time what the danger is.

"The men stood looking round them and pointing at the deserted holes. Neither of them was the farmer—we all knew what he looked like. He must have asked them to come and bring the body of the rabbit and then been too lazy to go out with them; just told them where to go, and they weren't too sure about the exact place. You could see that from the way they looked about.

"After a little, one of them trod out his white stick and started burning another, and then they went over to a hole and pushed the body right down it with a long pole. After that, they went away.

"We went away too—I can't remember how. Fescue was as good as mad: when we got back to Nutley Copse he just lay tharn in the first burrow he found and wouldn't come out next day or the day after. I don't know what happened to him in the end—I never saw him after that. Stitchwort and I managed to get hold of a burrow of our own later that summer, and we shared it for a long time. We never spoke of what we'd seen, even when we were alone together. Stitchwort was killed later, when the Efrafans attacked the warren.

"I know you all think I'm unfriendly. Perhaps you've been thinking I don't like anyone here—that I'm against you. It isn't that—now you know it isn't. Oh, what haunts me always is that I keep thinking . . . does that wretched rabbit have to go through it all again and again and again, forever? The stone—the pain . . . and might we too—"

The big, burly Coltsfoot lay sobbing like a kitten. Pipkin, too, was crying, and Hazel could feel Blackberry trembling against his side in the dark of the Honeycomb. Then Fiver spoke, with a quiet assurance that cut through the horror in the burrow like the calling of a plover across bare fields at night.

"No, Coltsfoot. That's not the way of it. It's true enough that there are many terrible and dangerous things in that land beyond, where you went with your friends that night; but in the end, however far away it may seem, Frith keeps his promise to El-ahrairah. I know this, and you can believe it. Those weren't real creatures that you saw. Only, in places where bad things have happened, sometimes a kind of strange force lingers on, like lonely pools of water after a storm; and now and then some of us fall into those pools. What you saw wasn't real—you said so yourself. It was an echo you heard, not a voice. And remember, it saved your warren that evening. Where else might that body have been put otherwise—and who can understand all that Frith knows and brings to pass?"

He was silent and, although Coltsfoot made no answer, himself said no more. Evidently he felt that Coltsfoot must take it from there on his own, without repetition or argument to convince him. After a little, the others dispersed to their sleeping burrows, leaving Coltsfoot and Fiver alone.

Coltsfoot did take it. For several days afterward, he was to be seen at silflay with Fiver, quietly browsing over the grass, talking and listening to his new friend.

As the bitter winter passed, his spirits gradually lightened, and by the following spring he had become quite a talkative and cheerful rabbit, not infrequently to be found telling stories to kittens under the bank.

"Fiver," said Bluebell one evening in early April, when the scent of the first violets was drifting under the new beech leaves, "do you think you could order a nice, gentle,

unfrightening sort of ghost for me? Only I've been thinking—they seem almost to do quite a bit of good in the long
run."

"The *very* long run," answered Fiver, "for those who
can run without stopping."

7

Speedwell's Story

It is a far, far better thing to have a firm anchor in nonsense
than to put out on the troubled seas of thought.

J. K. GALBRAITH, *The Affluent Society*

"Oh, you're always asking me for a story," said Dandelion, one evening in the Honeycomb when everyone had crowded in out of the April rain. "Why don't you ask someone else to tell a story? What about Speedwell there? He tells almost as many jokes as Bluebell, but I've never heard him tell a story yet. I'm sure all those jokes ought to add up to a story, that's if they're laid end to end properly. How about it, Speedwell?"

"Yes, yes," they all chorused. "Speedwell, tell us a story!"

"Well, all right," said Speedwell, as soon as he could make himself heard. "I *will* tell you a story, about an adventure I had last summer. But while I'm telling it, I don't want any rabbits interrupting or asking questions. The first rabbit who interrupts goes out into the rain. Is that agreed?"

They all agreed, chiefly out of curiosity to learn what

Speedwell was going to tell them, and when everyone had settled down comfortably, he began.

"It was one day toward the end of last summer, when the weather was terribly hot and dry, that I decided to go and get my fur cooled. I've always thought it's a great pity that rabbits can't take their fur off in hot weather, but at least it's a relief to go to the Cooler's."

Hawkbit was spluttering on the edge of a question. Speedwell stopped, and Hawkbit hurriedly swallowed what he had been going to say. Speedwell resumed.

"Well, so I set off down the hill to the field where the Iron Tree grows. But when I got there, I found that some-one had planted butterflies—blue ones—all over it, and I couldn't get it to do what I wanted. So I just lined up all the biggest butterflies I could see and told them to fly with me across to the farm.

"When we reached the farm, before we even came down, what should I see but a fox sitting up in the farmyard, eating the lettuces? I told the butterflies to attack it, but they were afraid to, so I just jumped down and went to find a bucket to put the fox in. I found the bucket, all right, hung up to dry on the clothesline, but some starlings had been using it for a nest, and I had to take it with all the nestlings in it, squeaking for food. I told them there was a nice, fresh fox all ready for them, but when they jumped out, they frightened the fox so much that it ran away, with all the nestlings chasing after it. I let them go and kept the bucket for myself.

"Well, I was playing with the bucket, rolling it backward and forward across the yard, when suddenly a badger looked out of it and asked what I thought I was doing, waking him up. I told him he couldn't have been there long, because I'd only just seen it empty myself, but he only said, 'Ho, we'll see about that!' and got out and began chasing me. Well, there was only one thing for it. I took off my head and sent it rolling away, down to the road, and the badger after it, gor-boom! gor-boom! Then I sat down where I was, and the farmer's little girl came out and brought me a big plateful of carrots."

At this point Bluebell said, "But—" Speedwell waited, but Bluebell turned it into a cough, and Speedwell went on.

"When I'd finished the carrots, I could hear a lot of scrabbling and stamping not far off, so I went to see what it was all about. And in the ditch I found a whole crowd of hedgehogs, all arguing which of them was the most prickly. I told them *I* was, and at that they all came for me, fairly bellowing with rage like a lot of sheep. I ran away as fast as I could, but all the same they'd have caught me if I hadn't suddenly come upon my head sitting in a puddle. I put it on again quick and looked really fiercely at those hedgehogs, so that they all rolled over one another trying to get away. I let them go and sat down for a rest.

"But would you believe it? Inside two and a half breaths of fresh air, down flies Kehaar and three of his mates, all asking where were they and what had happened to Bigwig. I told them Bigwig was busy climbing a tree to get out of the heat, but at that they all came up and sat down round me, asking was I sure I was telling the truth. That made me really cross, and I said to them they could be sure I'd never told the truth in my life. I wanted to get away from them, so I lifted myself up by my ears and climbed into a lettuce tree just behind me. I hid behind the lettuces and waited until the seagulls had all flown away. Then I ate every single lettuce I could find and three that I couldn't, just to make sure.

"When I came down, feeling a lot heavier, there was a beautiful stream of clear water running along beside a bed of roses and crocuses. So I picked a crocus—a nice, yellow one—jumped into it and sat down, and there I was, floating along without a care in the world, when all of a sudden I remembered that I'd been going to have my fur cooled. It wasn't far to the Cooler's, so I rammed my crocus up against the bank, told it to wait until I got back, and ran across the field. There were two horses grazing there, a green one and a sky-blue one, so I asked the green one to be so kind as to let me ride him as far as the Cooler's, and the sky-blue one said he'd be delighted, so off we went together."

At this moment Hawkbit was seized with a fit of coughing, through which could be heard occasional words —"nonsense"—"whoever"—"sky-blue horse." Speedwell waited politely until Hawkbit had finished coughing and then remarked, "Where was I? Oh, yes, of course.

"I really looked wonderful, riding on that sky-blue horse. All the blackbirds and pinkbirds for miles around came to look at us. We got to the Cooler's in no time, and I asked my sky-blue horse to wait outside.

"It was splendid at the Cooler's, and I soon felt a whole lot better. As soon as I'd got all the ice out of my fur, I went outside and whatever do you think? There were that fox and that badger sitting up together, talking to each other and saying all the nastiest things they could think of about *me*. I just picked them up and banged their two heads together so that they rang like a cuckoo in April. Then I jumped back on my beautiful sky-blue horse and we galloped away. 'Where to, master?' asks the horse. 'Well,' I said, 'I think we ought to go and see to my yellow crocus boat in the stream, if it's not too far.' 'Not too far, master?' says my horse. 'Why, we're there!' And so we were, only we'd been going backward, you see, and so of course I hadn't noticed.

"There was my boat, safe and sound. The horse got in and then I got in, and off we went upstream and down dale. Sure enough, there was the farmer's dear little daughter waiting for us on the bank, and I took her for a ride on my sky-blue horse.

"We went to the rabbits' meeting—oh, thousands and thousands of rabbits—and when they saw us, they all said, 'Let's make him our Chief—our King—and little Lucy shall be his Queen!'

"So there we were, King and Queen of the rabbits, and Lucy was covered with flowers and I was covered with dandelion leaves! I dug a nice hole for us to sleep in together, and I told her stories until she fell asleep. My horse slept too, but then his master came looking for him, and the farmer came looking for his Lucy. He had a whole bushel of hay with him, so my horse didn't go hungry, and my dear Lucy rode him all the way home to the farm, and I promised to come and see her every time it rained. It rained honey for her and lettuce leaves for me, and we fairly lived like the King and Queen we were.

> "Rabbits so clever
> As blue as the sky!
> Rabbits forever,
> A rabbit am I!

> "You take the left hand,
> I'll take the right.
> You be the black queen,
> I'll be the white!

"And that's the end of my story," said Speedwell.

PART II

8

The Story of the Comical Field

But as the night fell, he begun [*sic*] to be sensible of some
creature keeping pace with him and, as he thought, peering and
looking upon him from the next Alley to that he was in.

M. R. JAMES, "Mr. Humphreys and His Inheritance"

This (said Dandelion) is one of the many stories that
are told about the adventures of El-ahrairah and Rabscuttle
during their long return journey from the stone burrow of
the Black Rabbit of Inlé.

They went slowly, for both of them were exhausted and
badly shocked by their terrible experience. The weather,
however, was kind. Day after day was sunny and warm. El-
ahrairah used to sleep in the afternoons, while Rabscuttle
kept watch for any elil who might be about. But the days
were peaceful: there were no alarms or sudden escapes, and
gradually El-ahrairah began to recover some of his old energy and strength. The larks sang high and the blackbirds
sang low, and it seemed as though Lord Frith himself was
making it easy for them to rejoin the placid natural world
they thought of as their own.

One bright, clear evening, toward sunset, the two of them were lolloping gently across a hilltop, keeping an eye out, as they went, for some sheltered, safe place where they might be able to spend the night. Having come over the crest, they stopped to look at the land below and to choose their best way down.

It was exactly the kind of farming country they were used to: green fields—for it was early summer—and patches of woodland where the new leaves were glinting in the sun. Somewhere far off, a man was chugging about on a hrududu. All was as accustomed as could be—except for one curious feature, of a kind which neither of them had seen before.

Not far from a lonely-looking road stood a big house—smokeless chimneys, glassless windows and broken roofs. As any rabbit could perceive, it was in ruins and deserted, for there were no men anywhere around it. They could see the overgrown, jungly garden and the paths all covered with weeds. There were a few sheds here and there, and El-ahrairah was just thinking that one of them would make a good shelter for the night, when he noticed something else distinctly unusual.

On the nearer side of the garden, divided from it by a low wall, lay a piece of ground about the size of an ordinary meadow. It could in fact have been a meadow, except that it was all broken up into green paths, bordered by thick hedges running every which way. It lay empty in the westering sunshine, and although El-ahrairah remained looking at it for some time, he saw no sign of animals or birds.

"What do you suppose that is?" he asked Rabscuttle. "It's obviously some kind of man-thing, but I've never seen a place like it before, have you?"

"I don't know any more than you do, master," replied Rabscuttle. "It's no good to us, that's certain. We'd do best to let it alone, wouldn't we?"

"No, I'd like to have a closer look at it," replied El-ahrairah. "Let's go down that way. It can't do us any harm, and I'd like to know what on earth it's for. I can't see that it's any use at all, even to men."

They went slowly down the hillside, stopped for a bite of grass, made their way along a couple of hedgerows, and soon found themselves quite near what El-ahrairah had named "the comical field." There was no gate or any sort of entry that they could see, so El-ahrairah, more and more puzzled, led the way along one side.

"There must *be* a way in," he said to Rabscuttle, "or what's the good of it?"

Rabscuttle hadn't changed his first idea that they ought to let it alone, but the truth was that he was glad to see his master getting back some of his old spirits and evidently up for a bit of adventure or mischief, for he had been drained and low for many days since leaving the Black Rabbit. So he said nothing and followed obediently as El-ahrairah went along the hedge to the far end and turned the corner.

The first thing they saw when they got round the corner was a solitary rabbit feeding in a patch of short grass. His back was turned to them, and he took no notice as they

made their way up to him. As soon as he became aware of
them, he jumped and looked at them nervously. However,
he did not run away but remained where he was, only trembling a little as El-ahrairah greeted him and wished him
well. They could see now that he was old, with graying fur,
peering eyes and slow movements. In some curious way that
he could not pin down, El-ahrairah found himself not much
liking the look of him, but this, he thought, must be due to
one of the odd, confused spells that had been coming upon
him from time to time since leaving the Black Rabbit. He
knew he was not altogether himself, but he had grown accustomed to paying little attention to these intermittent
feelings.

The old rabbit told them that his name was Greenweed. He had lived here for a long time, he said. There
were no other rabbits now, and he was quite alone. El-
ahrairah asked him whether he wasn't afraid of elil, living so
solitarily, but he answered that no elil ever troubled him. "I
expect I'm too old and tough," he said. "I wouldn't be to
their taste." El-ahrairah could not tell whether this was
meant seriously or as a joke.

After sunset, when they were settling down together
for the night, El-ahrairah asked Greenweed about the big,
ruined house and whether he could remember a time when
men had lived there.

"Indeed I can," replied Greenweed. "Once, there used
to be any number of men."

"Why did they go?" asked El-ahrairah.

"That I can't tell," said he. "As I seem to recall, they went away a few at a time, until there was none left."

"And this strange place, this comical field of green paths: Do you know what it was for? What was the use of it?"

"It was of no practical use," answered Greenweed. "I've seen men go in there—wander about until they got to the middle, they used to—and then do their best to find their way out again. They did it just for sport; it was a kind of game they used to play. You ought to pay it a visit while you're here."

El-ahrairah was puzzled. "A game? That seems stupid."

"Well," said Greenweed, "that's only one of the stupid things men do to amuse themselves. If you'd lived as close to them as I have, you'd know that. But it's worth going into, all the same."

"Have *you* ever been in there?" asked El-ahrairah.

"Oh, yes; often, when I was young; but it's of no use to a rabbit."

"Well," said El-ahrairah, "perhaps we might take a look round it tomorrow, before we go on, as long as the weather stays fine and it doesn't rain."

The next morning was as fine as ever, and El-ahrairah and Rabscuttle began the day by finding their way into the deserted, overgrown garden. They were hoping that they might find something good to eat, but even in the vegetable garden they came upon nothing to attract them.

"It looks as though a lot of other rabbits have been

here before us, master," said Rabscuttle. "We might as well leave it to the mice and the birds."

"Yes, we'll go back now," said El-ahrairah, "and see what we can find in that comical field."

"Somehow or other I don't much like that field," said Rabscuttle, "but I can't tell why."

"It's only because it's new to you," said El-ahrairah. "Natural rabbit suspicion. Anyhow, we won't stay there long. We have to be on our way."

Greenweed was waiting to encourage them and see them off. He showed them the way in and came a few yards with them into the comical field.

"Is there any particular way we ought to go to get to the middle?" asked El-ahrairah.

"Not that I know of," said Greenweed. "As I understood it, that was what the men found amusing. They had to find their own way in and out. If they got confused, that was all part of the game."

After he had left them they sat for a while, puzzling over which way to go. Finally they decided that one way was as good as another, and set off down one of the green paths leading between the hedges. For some time they seemed to be going round and round, and were beginning to find it monotonous. They were on the point of deciding to go back, when they unexpectedly found themselves at the center. There was a big, upright stone in the middle of a little grassy square, and to one side an old wooden seat.

"This must be the center, all right," said El-ahrairah,

"because there's only one way in. We may as well lie in the sun for a bit before we go back."

They browsed awhile on the grass and then went to sleep in the sun. It was quiet and peaceful, and although El-ahrairah woke once or twice, he soon dropped off again.

When they finally woke, the sun had gone in. It was late in the afternoon and turning chilly.

"We'd better get back as quick as we can," said El-ahrairah. "That Greenweed'll be wondering where we've got to. We'd better stay the night with him now, and go on tomorrow."

They had supposed it would be easy to get out, but they soon found that it was nothing of the kind. They had no idea which way to go and wandered up and down the green paths until they felt quite bewildered.

It was during one of their puzzled halts that El-ahrairah became sure of something of which he had already been half aware for some time past. There was some other creature in the comical field as well as themselves—someone on the move like them. He could hear it: now far off; now, so it seemed, close by. This disturbed him, for rabbits, as you all know, by nature tend to be afraid of anything unfamiliar and particularly of any strange creature nearby which they cannot hear or see clearly. He and Rabscuttle remained perfectly still, staring at each other. They both felt alarmed.

"Should we join it, do you think?" asked El-ahrairah after a while. "It might be able to show us the way out."

"Don't make any mistake, master," replied Rabscuttle. "I don't know who or what it is, but I know it's searching for us, and if it finds us it means to kill us. We're being hunted."

They both began to run then: a panic flight, one way and another, not knowing where they were going. It was like a nightmare, a flight without direction or purpose, against all rabbit nature. For as you all know, in the normal way a rabbit knows where the danger lies or where the enemy is, and runs in the opposite direction. But here, among the paths of the comical field, they could not tell where the danger lay; nor could they run directly away from their pursuer, for every path twisted, came to a dead end or turned back on itself. For all they knew, they might be running straight toward this unknown enemy, the dread of whom clutched at their hearts more direly with every moment that passed. Up and down, back and forth, they ran, feeling not only helplessness and terror but also growing exhaustion.

At last, in the gathering darkness, they sank down together in a place where one of the hedges ended, leaving a gap which led into a straight path beyond.

"I can't go any further, master," gasped Rabscuttle. "I'm worn out. And look, we're going in circles. We've been this way before. There's the hraka I passed, on the ground."

At this, El-ahrairah realized the utter futility of their flight. He turned his head to look back at the way they had come, and it was at this moment that he saw for the first time, behind them, their approaching pursuer.

In afteryears El-ahrairah would never describe what he saw, and only once did he ever speak of it. This was when some rabbit once said to him, "But you saw and talked with the Black Rabbit of Inlé. How could this be worse?"

"The Black Rabbit," replied El-ahrairah, "inspired a terrible, indescribable awe: helplessness and the fear of endless darkness. But he is not wicked, evil or cruel." And not a word more would he say.

As the dreadful, malignant horror broke into a run upon seeing him, El-ahrairah dashed through the gap beside them, with Rabscuttle hard on his heels. And there they saw before them the way out, which they must have overlooked when they came along that path earlier.

"If that way out didn't move of its own accord," Rabscuttle used to say, "I'd still be ready to believe it did. I'd believe anything of that place."

Once out, they ran fast over the open grass, yet instinctively they knew that they would not be pursued further. "It won't go beyond its own place," said El-ahrairah.

Soon they saw Greenweed at silflay by himself in the last light. As they came up to him he jumped, stared at them with a kind of terrified incredulity and tried to run away. El-ahrairah pinned him down.

"So it didn't work for once, Greenweed," he said. "You contemptible, lying creature. It's all clear enough now. That—that wicked being has allowed you to live here and protected you from the elil to suit himself. It was your business to seem to befriend any rabbits who came this way and encourage them to go into that place, simply for amusement, as they supposed. Then, when they had gone in, you told your master."

The wretched Greenweed answered him never a word. He plainly thought El-ahrairah was going to kill him.

"Well, you won't do it anymore," said El-ahrairah at length. "You'll come with us tomorrow and we'll find somewhere else for you to live out your days like a decent rabbit."

Greenweed set out with them next day, and they left him in the first warren they came to. El-ahrairah said nothing to its Chief Rabbit about Greenweed's despicable treachery, saying only that he was too old to journey with them. They never heard any more of him.

9

The Story of the Great Marsh

He brought me up also out of an horrible pit, out of the miry
clay, and set my feet upon a rock, and established my goings.

PSALM 40:2

It was not long after dawn on a fine, clear morning
close to midsummer. El-ahrairah and Rabscuttle were making their way over a low saddle between two hills of the
grassy country they were crossing on their journey home.
Clumps of oxeye daisies were already in bloom here and
there, and there were patches of mauve sainfoin. As they
stopped to nibble the fresh grass, a light breeze began to
blow, bringing from below scents of sheep and river plants.

Ahead of them lay the kind of country with which they
were familiar. On the sunset side, however, the fields were
bordered by marshland, extending north as far as they could
see. A man was at work cutting reeds, but otherwise the
whole valley was still and quiet.

The rabbits, descending unhurriedly, came to a field
that lay near the marsh and ended on the opposite side in a
long bank topped by a hedge of hawthorn and elder. In this

were a number of rabbit holes, and as they reached it two rabbits came out and halted, watching their approach. El-ahrairah greeted them and remarked on the fine weather.

"Hlessil, are you?" said one of the rabbits. The other stared at El-ahrairah's mutilated ears but said nothing.

"Yes, I suppose we are," replied El-ahrairah. "We've been wandering for quite some time, but now we could do with a few days' rest. Do you think we might be allowed to stay here? I like the look of this warren, and if it's not over-crowded, perhaps no one would mind if we stopped for a bit."

"That'll be for our Chief to say, of course," replied the second rabbit. "Would you like to come and meet him? I shouldn't think he'll mind you staying. He's very easygoing as a rule."

The rabbits made their way along the bank, stopping beside a group of four or five holes at the further end.

"This is where our Chief's usually to be found," said the first rabbit. "I'll go in and tell him you're here. His name's Burdock, by the way," he added before disappearing down the nearest of the holes.

Burdock, when he came out to meet them, immediately struck El-ahrairah favorably. His manner was not at all unfriendly, and he seemed to think it only natural that a couple of hlessil should want to stay in his warren for a while.

"We have hardly any trouble with elil here," he said, "and so far we've been left alone by men. I suppose you've come from quite a long way off, haven't you? No other warrens anywhere near here, as far as I know. You can certainly stay here as long as you like."

El-ahrairah and Rabscuttle settled in comfortably and found the warren so much to their liking that they felt in no particular hurry to move on. The rabbits were as friendly and sociable as anyone could wish. Burdock in particular showed himself glad of the visitors' company and of the opportunity to learn more from them about the world they had come from. He and several of his Owsla often came to silflay beside them of an evening, and would ask them to tell of their adventures "out in the Beyond."

In his replies, El-ahrairah was always careful to say nothing about the Black Rabbit, and as their hosts were too polite to ask about his mutilated ears, he was able to avoid the whole subject of their reason for wandering and of whether they had any particular destination in mind. They obviously felt respect both for him and for Rabscuttle as rabbits who had traveled far and wide and survived all manner of perils.

"I could never have done all you've done," said Celandine, the captain of Owsla, as they lay on the bank together one sunny evening. "I like to feel safe, myself. I've never felt any wish to go anywhere outside this warren."

"Well, none of you have ever been driven to it, have you?" replied Rabscuttle. "You've certainly been lucky there."

"Why, have *you* been driven to it?" asked Celandine.

Rabscuttle, catching a warning glance from El-ahrairah, merely answered, "Well, you could say so," and, as Celandine did not press him, left it at that.

It was past sunset one evening a few days later, and most of the rabbits were about to end silflay and settle in for the night, when yet another hlessi, a total stranger, came limping along the bank and asking to be taken to the Chief Rabbit. When it was suggested to him that he might stop and feed first, he became frantic, insisting that his news was urgent, a matter of life and death. Then he collapsed on the grass, apparently exhausted. Someone went to tell Burdock, who came at once, accompanied by El-ahrairah, Rabscuttle and Celandine. At first they could not bring the stranger round at all, but after a time he opened his eyes, sat up and asked which was the Chief Rabbit. Burdock told him kindly to take his time before trying to talk, but this only agitated him still further.

"Rats," he panted. "The rats are coming. Thousands of rats. Killers."

"Coming here, do you mean?" asked Burdock. "Where are they coming from? Are you saying we're in danger from them? We're not afraid of rats as a rule."

"Yes," answered the hlessi. "Your whole warren's in danger. You're all in deadly peril. This is a mass migration of rats. They're not more than a single day away from here. They're killing every creature they find in their way. It was long before dawn this morning—it was in the middle of last night—when all of us—every rabbit in our warren—woke up to find them in among us. No one had heard or smelled them coming. Some of us tried to fight, but it was impossible. There were a thousand rats to every rabbit. Some of us did our best to clear out and run, but I think I must have been the only rabbit who managed it. I couldn't see much in the dark, but when I got outside I couldn't hear any other rabbits. There were rats everywhere—every rat in the world, you'd have thought. There was no chance of looking for other rabbits. I simply ran. As it was, I had to run right through a whole crowd of them. I've got bites all over my legs. I don't know how on earth I managed to get clear. One moment I was kicking and biting—just frantically, no thought of anything except that I was terrified—and the next I realized they'd apparently left off and I was alone in the grass. I'm afraid I didn't stop to look for other rabbits, and neither would you. But later—a long time later—I looked down from where I'd got to and saw the rats down below me, crowds of them, coming this way. You couldn't see the grass for rats. I'd say they're bound to be here by tomorrow. Your only chance is to get out, and quickly."

Burdock turned to Celandine with a look of dismay and uncertainty.

"What are we to do, do you think?"

But Celandine seemed equally daunted.

"I don't know. Whatever you say, Chief Rabbit."

"Should we call a meeting of the Owsla and put it to them?"

At this, El-ahrairah, who had so far said nothing, felt that he must interpose.

"Chief Rabbit, you haven't got the time to spare for a meeting. The rats will almost certainly be here before ni-Frith tomorrow. You've got to go, and quickly too."

"If our rabbits will come," said Burdock. "They may refuse. They haven't heard anything about rats yet."

"You've got no choice," said El-ahrairah.

"But where can we go?" asked Celandine. "On two sides of this warren there's a river much too broad to swim. The rats would catch our rabbits on the bank. And on the sunset side there's nothing but the marsh."

"How wide is that?" asked El-ahrairah.

"None of us know. No one's ever crossed it. It wouldn't be possible to cross it. There are no paths. It's all pools and quagmires. We'd only sink in the mud. But the rats wouldn't. They're so much lighter, you see."

"Well, from what you've told me, I think we'll have to try. Chief Rabbit, I'll undertake to lead them through the marsh myself, if you'll back me up and tell them they've got to follow me."

"And what in Frith's name do *you* know about it?" said Celandine angrily. "A brainless hlessi, who's only been here a few days."

"Well, please yourself," said El-ahrairah. "You haven't suggested anything else, and I'm ready to do my best for you."

Then Burdock and Celandine began arguing with each

other to no purpose whatever, impelled, as El-ahrairah could see, by nothing but their own fear and by a sort of panic-stricken notion that if only they could go on talking, something would happen.

"Rabscuttle," he said quietly, "go round everywhere as quick as you can and tell the rabbits about the rats. Then tell them that you and I are going to guide them across the marsh and that we'll be starting fu Inlé. Tell them they're all to meet me by that plane tree over there—do you see the one I mean?—and that there's no time to lose. If some of them say they won't come, you can't stand about arguing. You'll just have to leave them. And above all, don't let them think you're afraid. Act as calm and confident as you can."

Rabscuttle touched his nose to El-ahrairah's and was off on the instant. El-ahrairah turned back to Burdock and Celandine, interrupted their argument and told them what he had done. He had expected them to blame and condemn him, perhaps even to attack him and beat him up, but to his surprise they did nothing of the kind. They were sulky and would not give him their approval, but he could tell that inwardly they were glad to have responsibility for the frightening business taken off their backs. If it all went wrong, which they clearly thought it would, they could blame him, but if he succeeded against all likelihood, they could say that they had given him the authority to do his best.

To El-ahrairah, it seemed to take an age for the news to spread over the whole warren; and then more trouble began. Rabbits came from all sides to talk to Burdock, to

Celandine and to himself. Some did not believe in the danger and said they would not join with those who were leaving. Others—and these were does—said they had newborn kittens in their burrows and what were they to do? To these he could only reply that if they wanted to save their lives, they must leave their litters and follow him, at which they grew angry. Others again asked him how far it was across the marsh and how long it would take to cross it. He answered that he did not know but was determined to save their lives if he could.

After some time he collected Rabscuttle and went across to the plane tree. He was surprised to find a great many rabbits waiting for him, among them Burdock and Celandine. He spoke to them as encouragingly as he could and praised them for making the right decision—to come with him. Then, as the moon began to rise at his back, he set off without hesitation into the marsh.

Now, the truth was that El-ahrairah knew a little more about marshes than most rabbits, for he had once lived in the dreary marshes of Kelfazin. He had realized that to cross this marsh was the only chance for these rabbits and that since their Chief Rabbit could not, he himself would have to lead them. But he had not thought at all about what this would actually be like. Now, almost at once, he began to learn. He had gone only a little way into the marsh when he started to cross a patch of open ground and suddenly found himself sinking to the full length of his front paws. He pulled back just in time and bumped up against

Burdock, whom he had told to follow him, so that it might at least seem to the rabbits that their Chief was leading them. He paused, considering, and then tried a few steps to his left. Again he found himself sinking and drew back. To his right, then? Thinking that it would be no better, he forced himself to try it. This time he went further before the ground gave way beneath him. He pulled himself clear, lay down and rolled completely over to one side, once and then twice before standing up. The ground was firm.

He waited for Burdock and Celandine to join him and then set off along the edge of the ground where he had begun to sink. After covering some distance he turned again to his left, trying the ground step by step. This time he did not sink, and allowed himself to hope that he might have gone round the edge of the quagmire. If he had, he thought, he might be able to start going forward again, keeping the moon behind him.

He went very cautiously, trying every patch of ground before putting his weight on it. Sometimes the ground bore him, and sometimes his paws sank in almost before he could withdraw them. Now that the full moon was giving him more light, he looked ahead very carefully, trying to see whether there was any difference, however slight, between safe and unsafe ground; but he could see no difference at all. Sniffing, however, proved another matter. The drier ground had a different smell from the swamp, and by nosing his way he was able to make a little headway, though only slowly and often crookedly. His westward advance was minimal, for often he had to go a long distance to right or left before once more inching his way forward. Once, he came upon a kind of broad, muddy pond, its standing water deep and still enough to reflect the moonlight. He went a long way round it, guessing that the edges would be nothing but watery mud.

After what seemed half the night, he began to feel himself tiring. Constantly pulling his paws back out of the mire was bad enough, but on top of this was the continual strain of smelling and probing every foot of ground before entrusting his weight to it. How far across the marsh had they really gone, and anyway how wide was the marsh? He guessed now that they would not have crossed it by sunrise and would still be in it next day—perhaps all day and the next night as well. The rabbits would have to rest, and their rest could only be in the open, with not even a bush or a hedge for cover. They wouldn't like that, and neither would he. When and if they came out of the marsh, what sort of a place would they come to?

He broke off these reflections to resume concentration on his next step. That was still the only way, he thought: one step, and then another, and another, and constantly pulling his paws back just in time. Twice he disturbed moorhens, which flew angrily and noisily away, no doubt feeling it against all nature that rabbits—rabbits!—should be here in the middle of the night.

In aftertimes, El-ahrairah used to say that of all his adventures, this crossing of the marsh by night was the worst. Several times he thought that he would never get out of it alive. In a way he felt glad that there was no choice but to struggle on, because if there had been, he would have taken it without hesitation. The moon showed nothing on all sides but a desolate, empty place, fraught everywhere with horrible danger and offering no shelter or refuge at all. His body would not take long to sink under the slime, he thought. And what then? Rabscuttle would have to take over. He had better give him some instruction.

When they set out, he had placed Rabscuttle in the rear, to look after stragglers and dropouts. He sent a message back down the line for him to come up and join him. Rabscuttle seemed to be a lifetime coming. When at last he appeared, El-ahrairah asked him what it was like at the back. How were the rabbits doing?

"Better than I'd feared," said Rabscuttle. "No one's actually dropped out and had to be left behind. All of them still feel sure that they're going to get there—wherever it is. And as luck would have it, they've got a good storyteller. Rabbit name of Chicory. He's kept going with one story after another. So they don't drop out, because they want to know what happens next, you see. Anyway, what can I do to help you, master?"

El-ahrairah explained, and stayed with Rabscuttle until he was sure he had got the idea. Then he left him to sniff his way forward, and remained to watch the rabbits go past. Rabscuttle, he thought, had been right. They were for the most part in good heart and certainly not tired out by simply going where they were led. His own fatigue and low spirits he could attribute only to the load of responsibility he had taken on himself: that, and the labor of sounding out the way, of finding dangerous ground and pulling back from it in time. He waited for Chicory and was amused to hear that he was telling the story of the King's Lettuce. At the far end of the column he found a small, very young rabbit, who was having difficulty in keeping up. He encouraged him warmly and accompanied him for a short distance before returning to Rabscuttle and Burdock.

Rabscuttle, as he had expected, was fully up to the unpleasant job and doing very well—better than himself, he thought. He seemed to find it positively amusing when his front paws sank into the mud. He obviously did not think he was in any danger or, if he did, was concealing it very well. What was more, he seemed to be on excellent terms with Burdock and Celandine, and had even allowed Celandine to take over from himself for a short time. "Nothing to it, nothing to it," he kept saying, and "Oops!" when Celandine went in up to his shoulders.

Soon the sky behind them began to lighten as daylight returned after the short summer night. When the sun rose, El-ahrairah looked ahead in the hope of seeing whatever lay on the other side of the marsh, but could see nothing except the same dismal wilderness. How long, he wondered, before they began to feel hungry and exhausted? If a whole day in the marsh lay before them, they would probably begin to split up into groups of the strong and not-so-strong; and, worse, to try to find food for themselves, wandering here and there. That would be fatal. He told Burdock and Celandine of his anxiety and suggested that they should fall back among their rabbits and do all they could to keep them together. "If only they'll do as I say," said Celandine. "They've all got used to pleasing themselves about that, you know. The truth is, we've had it far too easy for far too long." To this El-ahrairah could think of no answer.

He was just about to take over the lead from Rabscuttle when a heron flew down nearby and began wading beside them. It was not disposed to be friendly. "What on earth are you wretched rabbits doing here?" it squawked to Rabscuttle. "This marsh belongs to me and my family. We don't want you rabbits here. Why don't you get out?"

El-ahrairah explained that this was exactly what they were trying to do. He told the heron about the rats and about their forced march by night.

"You mean you want to get out as soon as you can?" asked the heron. "If that's all you want, I'll be glad enough to show you the way."

"We'd be more than happy to be guided by you," said El-ahrairah. "But don't forget that we can't wade, and mud you think of as safe, with your long legs, is deadly dangerous for us. Have we far to go to get out?"

"Not far," replied the heron tersely.

"That's the best news I've ever heard," said El-ahrairah.

He himself took up a position immediately behind the heron, and as he had feared, it proved dangerous. In spite of what he had said, the heron simply did not understand that the rabbits could not wade, and when El-ahrairah tried to explain this, it grew first impatient and then angry. At last, after quietly enduring its insults and abuse for some considerable time, he persuaded it to lead them over ground into which they would not sink and to avoid places treacherous to rabbits though not to itself. Once it had grasped the difference, the heron's guidance proved helpful, though not altogether reliable. Its manner remained sharp and unfriendly, and El-ahrairah thought it felt that a few rabbits drowned in the bog would be neither here nor there. Its contempt for them was plain, and it was all El-ahrairah could do to keep his temper.

They did make progress, however, and went faster than before; and he was forced to admit to himself that they went safely over ground which he would never have trusted solely on his own account. In spite of what the heron had said, they seemed to go a very long way. At ni-Frith they were still struggling among the reeds and tussocks, without a sign of anything better. El-ahrairah's gnawing dilemma was that he dared not entrust the leadership to anyone else, even to the almost exhausted Rabscuttle, and dared not a second time leave the front and drop back to encourage the rabbits and keep them up together. He himself felt as tired as he had ever been in his life, and in spite of Rabscuttle's best efforts to conceal it, he could tell that he, too, was almost worn out. So what sort of shape could the other rabbits be in? He told Rabscuttle to wait for the last ones to reach him and then report what things were like at the back.

He begged the heron to stop while they had a rest, but it did so with such bad grace that he feared it would leave them.

"Why can't your confounded rabbits fly?" it asked. "You'd be out of here directly if you could fly, like any reasonable creature."

"I only wish we could," replied El-ahrairah, "but it can only be by the will of Lord Frith that we can't."

At this moment, he found Rabscuttle beside him. "Master, there are two rabbits missing. And now they're nearly all in pretty poor shape down at the back."

Would the whole band fall to pieces? wondered El-ahrairah. They had better get on before it did. He begged the heron to be so kind as to continue.

Then, in no time at all, or so it seemed, he saw a line of horse chestnut trees topping a green bank well above their own level. Soon they were scrambling upward, and the ground beneath their paws was dry. "We're across, aren't we?" he asked the heron. "We're out of the marsh?"

"Yes," replied the heron. "Don't ever come back, will you?" And so saying, without waiting to be thanked, it flew away, mounting with great, slow strokes of its heavy wings.

El-ahrairah was up the bank in no time. The exposed roots of one of the chestnuts were bone dry under his paws. Rabscuttle was beside him. He had never felt so deeply relieved.

The next rabbit he saw was Burdock, sitting nearby to watch his rabbits as they clambered out of the marsh and up the bank. Burdock might have been a useless Chief Rabbit in a crisis, but now he showed that there was another side to him. He knew all his rabbits by name and greeted each one, congratulating him or her and praising their courage and determination. And they, for their part, showed plainly enough that they liked and respected him. He spoke, too, about the rabbits who were missing, and was clearly very sorry for their loss. "Yarrow and Kingcup," he said to El-ahrairah with obvious regret and sorrow. "Two of the best rabbits in the warren. We could have spared almost anyone but those two." El-ahrairah, who had not troubled himself to learn many of the rabbits' names, felt ashamed.

Climbing the bank, they found themselves on the edge of a wide, luxuriant meadow where the tall midsummer grass had not yet been cut. The exhausted rabbits crept into it, ate and at once fell asleep. "Let them do as they please," said Burdock. "They've earned it." El-ahrairah saw no reason to disagree.

10

The Story of the Terrible Hay-Making

In nature there are no rewards or punishments:
there are consequences.

HORACE ANNESLEY VACHELL, *The Face of Clay*

Most of the rabbits remained sleeping or resting in the long grass of the meadow until early morning of the following day. But before that, on the previous evening, El-ahrairah and Rabscuttle had been awake and looking over the surroundings. The first and most obvious thing, on which they were strongly in agreement, was that they were too close to a farmhouse and its yard and barns.

"I don't know what they'll decide to do," said El-ahrairah, "but they can't stay here for long, that's certain. A sudden invasion by a whole bunch of rabbits quite nearby—that's something the farm people are going to notice at once. And you know what that means: guns, dogs, even poison, perhaps—downright persecution, anyway. They'll have to get away from here."

"What, back through the marsh, master?" asked Rabscuttle. "Surely they wouldn't do it, would they?"

"Well, if they do, it'll be without you and me," replied El-ahrairah. "We have to be getting on with our little stroll home."

At this moment they were joined by Burdock and Celandine, who were full of praise and gratitude for the part El-ahrairah and Rabscuttle had played in the crossing of the marsh.

"We could never have done it without you," said Burdock.

"Do you mean to go back?" asked El-ahrairah. "I suppose the rats must have come through and gone by now."

Burdock was emphatic that nothing would induce him to go back across the marsh. "And I'm sure that goes for all of us," he said. "There'd be no point in it. I haven't really gone all round here yet, but there seem to be masses of food and just about everything rabbits could possibly wish for. There's a whole vegetable garden just along there, for a start."

"Well, it's not for me to advise you," said El-ahrairah. "We're just a couple of wandering hlessil. But do you mind me asking—have you had much experience of human beings and what they do to rabbits?"

"No, I haven't," answered Burdock. "I've hardly ever seen a human being, and I certainly haven't been near any. But rabbits can hide and rabbits can run. They can run a lot faster than human beings, I know that."

"True enough," said El-ahrairah. "But all the same, this place, where we are now, is too close to that farmhouse, and if you let your rabbits settle here and go traipsing in and out of that kitchen garden, you'll be letting them in for danger and death. Human beings hate all rabbits, and they're nearly always ready to kill them wherever they are, but rabbits in a vegetable garden they'll go to a whole lot of trouble to kill, believe me."

"Well, but I don't think I could stop my rabbits going in," said Burdock evasively. "What do you want me to do?"

"Look," said El-ahrairah, "I'm not Chief Rabbit and not trying to be. I'm just a passing visitor. But if you want my advice, I think you ought to take them off into open country, right away from the farm. Edge of a wood, an open hillside, somewhere like that. It's just that I *know* there'll be a whole lot of trouble if they stay here. Anyway," he went on, as Celandine came up and joined them, "let's all have a look round together and get ourselves an idea of the place, shall we?"

During the morning the four rabbits went over the farmland from end to end. It was very well tended and prosperous. There was a big field of cows and another of sheep, with all the hedges and fences very sound and efficiently maintained. There was another, bare field where the hay had already been cut and the ricks built. At its far end, cornfields, planted some with wheat and some with barley, extended out as far as distant woodland.

Coming back, they went through an orchard of young cherry trees, some way away from the vegetable garden. Burdock was looking for a convenient gap, when they smelled tobacco and heard a man approaching from the other side of the hedge. They were just in time to hide among some nearby nut-bushes before he came out through a small gate and set off toward the long-grass meadow where they had spent the night. As he tossed his white stick into the grass, a rabbit bolted almost under his feet. He stopped and watched it disappear among the scrubland and bushes bordering the orchard.

"See what I mean?" said Burdock. "Rabbits can run and rabbits can hide."

That afternoon, when El-ahrairah and Rabscuttle were alone together, Rabscuttle said, "Do you think we'd do best to leave these rabbits now, master, before the trouble begins? Only at this rate, there's bound to be a whole lot of trouble, isn't there? And quite soon, I'd say. We don't want to be mixed up in it."

"You're probably right," answered El-ahrairah, "but I haven't altogether given up hope of getting them to see sense. If I can't, then I promise you we'll leave as quick as we can."

After a few days, virtually all the rabbits had discovered the vegetable garden for themselves. There were two or three ways into it, and near these, on both sides of the hedge, conspicuous rabbit paths had already begun to appear. El-ahrairah, forbidding Rabscuttle to risk his life anywhere near the garden, went in himself one fine evening toward sunset, to see what sort of a state it was in. He found the lettuces nibbled to nothing and the cabbages and cauliflowers showing all too plainly the effect of the rabbits' attentions. As he had expected, a good deal more had been spoiled than had been eaten. Finding a couple of youngsters among the carrots, he tried to tell them about their danger, but they had no mind to listen to him.

"Why, I think Celandine's in here himself," said one of them. "We know how to get away quick enough if any men come along. This place is far too good to let alone. I'd never imagined there *could* be flayrah like this."

At night, most of the rabbits slept or lay up among the long grass of the meadow alongside the marsh. The fine weather continued without a hint of rain, and the only rabbits to do any digging were two or three does who knew themselves to be pregnant and going to give birth to litters. The loose earth and other signs of their digging, in the bank leading down to the marsh, were clearly to be seen and added to El-ahrairah's anxiety. He noticed, too, that Burdock and Celandine did not seem to like his company as much as formerly, and he had little doubt of the reason. Even if he did not actually talk about the vegetable garden, his manner had become constrained by the constant thought of it, whereas every other rabbit except Rabscuttle lived in a state of almost riotous high spirits and well-being.

One afternoon, as he was lying in the sun, El-ahrairah saw two rabbits nearby setting off with a purposeful air in a direction opposite to that leading to the vegetable garden. He wondered what they might be up to, and followed them with as unconcerned an air as he could assume. He saw them go down the further end of the bank and make their way into the cherry orchard. He waited for a time and then went in himself, by a way different from theirs. He soon caught sight of them again and saw what they were doing. They were stripping the bark low down on one of the cherry trees. One or two trees nearby had been stripped already. And that was not all. At the far end of the orchard, two men were talking together as they walked slowly among the trees.

El-ahrairah went back to the meadow and began asking every rabbit he met where he could find Burdock. At length he came upon him asleep in one of the nestlike refuges the rabbits had made in the long grass. He woke him up and told him what he had seen.

"Well," said Burdock, "what do you expect me to do? I couldn't stop them even if I wanted to. They wouldn't leave the trees alone just because I told them."

"But don't you realize," said El-ahrairah, "that barking kills the trees and that the men are bound to notice and do everything they can to—"

Burdock stood up and faced El-ahrairah. He had clearly lost his temper. "Do you think I'm going to be ordered about by the likes of you, a ragamuffin hlessi who's lost his tail and ears and works himself into a fright about every single thing he sees? You're nothing but a continual nuisance. You'd better take care I don't tell Celandine to have you set upon and finished with. You think because you led the way through the marsh you can tell us all what to do and lay down the law about everything."

"Very well," replied El-ahrairah quietly. "I won't bother you anymore."

When El-ahrairah said this he meant it, but that was before the cat.

The cat, black-and-white and short-furred, made its first appearance about two days later, in the early evening. It came wandering slowly down from the vicinity of the farm-house, pausing from time to time and looking here and there at anything which attracted its momentary attention. Soon it reached the edge of the field of long grass and began walking along the verge, evidently with no particular pur-pose, for it went slowly and almost paw by paw. It wore a thin leather collar and had a sleek, well-fed appearance. It was certainly not hunting.

El-ahrairah and Rabscuttle were dozing together on the bank above the marsh when they became aware of the cat's approach. They both grew alert and held themselves in readiness for instant flight. The cat, however, passed within a few yards without paying them the least attention. All the same, thought El-ahrairah, it might be as well to move a lit-tle further away. He was just about to do so when he found Celandine beside him.

Celandine was holding himself tensely. He was breath-ing fast and watching the cat with a vigilant, aggressive air.

After a little, he said to El-ahrairah, "Do you see that damned pest out there?"

"Yes, of course," replied El-ahrairah.

"We're going to kill it," said Celandine.

"This year or next?" asked El-ahrairah, joining in what he took to be some kind of game.

"You don't believe me?" replied Celandine. "You may as well know that it won't be the first time our Owsla have killed a cat."

"I've never heard of rabbits attacking a cat," said El-ahrairah, "except perhaps a doe defending her litter."

"When we were living in the warren where you first joined us," said Celandine, "there was a cat which used to come hunting about and making a nuisance of itself, and after a bit our Owsla set upon it and killed it. That was when Betony was captain of Owsla and I was still quite young."

"And what happened?" asked El-ahrairah.

"What d'you mean, what happened?" answered Celandine.

"Did any human beings come looking for it? Did any of them take the body away?"

"No, nothing like that," said Celandine. "Rats disposed of the body, I suppose. Something did, anyway."

"And you want to show you're as good as Betony, and kill that cat?"

"Certainly. Three or four of my Owsla are mad keen."

"Well," said El-ahrairah, "I beg you, I implore you, to listen to me before you do anything else. From all you've told me, the cat your Captain Betony killed must have been a stray. It didn't belong to any human beings. It was just wandering on its own. But that cat out there belongs to the farmhouse. It's wearing a collar and it obviously gets plenty to eat. And it reeks of human beings. I could smell it from here when it went past just now. Drive it away by all means if you want to, but if you kill it the farmhouse human beings will come after you with everything they've got. As far as they're concerned, it'll be the last straw. You've ruined the vegetable garden and done a lot of damage in the cherry orchard. I'm surprised they haven't done their best to wipe you out already. Do take my advice, Celandine. Let the cat alone, for Frith's sake."

"I'll think about it," replied Celandine. "But the cat's asking for trouble, you must admit."

During the next two or three days, Celandine and three of his Owsla waited patiently in the long grass for the black-and-white cat, but it did not reappear. It was not until early evening several days later that it came sauntering along the verge and pausing to look here and there, as it had before.

From Celandine's point of view, the opportunity could not have been a better one. The cat lay down in the sun almost opposite where they were concealed, turned on its back and began washing its stomach. When the four rabbits leaped upon it, it was taken completely by surprise.

It fought, however, miawling and biting savagely. Its claws were more effective than the rabbits', and it was more used to using them. If it had not been for the reckless audacity of Celandine, it would almost certainly have got away. But lying on its back when he attacked it, it offered him the chance to use a rabbit's strongest weapon, its back legs. Leaping, Celandine landed on its chest, drove one of his back legs into its belly and kicked backward. This was decisive. Ripped open, horribly wounded, its guts trailing, it still struggled, scratching fiercely and clenching its teeth on Celandine's throat until he lay virtually at its mercy. But at this moment its strength failed. Gasping, it rolled over on its side and a few moments later lay dead. Celandine and his rabbits, covered with its blood and a great deal of their own, made off into the long grass.

It was almost dark before a girl from the farm found the body and, weeping bitterly, carried it away, all bloody as it was.

El-ahrairah did not himself see Celandine and his rabbits kill the cat; but Rabscuttle, who did, told him, and he also saw the weeping girl carry the body away.

"Shall we leave now, master?" asked Rabscuttle. "You surely don't want us to be mixed up with this place any longer, do you? We might be shot or . . . or . . . well, whatever the men are going to do."

"Yes, we'll leave, all right," replied El-ahrairah. "But I'm not ready yet. Just keep a lookout and tell me at once if you see the men doing anything unusual."

However, nothing happened on the following day and nothing the day after that. It was unusually early on the morning of the third day after the cat had been killed that Rabscuttle woke El-ahrairah and told him that a whole lot of men were coming into the long-grass field, most of them carrying sticks and one of them with a gun. El-ahrairah crept under a hawthorn bush to a place where both of them could watch the men, who at that moment were doing nothing except standing about, burning white sticks in their mouths and talking.

After some time, two of them went away and came back riding on the hrududu, pulling the grass cutter behind it. They drove it to a place at the outer edge of the long grass and began cutting the whole field in a circle, always going a little further inward as they came round. Meanwhile, the other men spread out and stood all round the edge, moving slowly inward as the grass was cut. Although El-ahrairah knew that the whole field was full of rabbits, he saw none come out. He realized that they wanted to stay hidden in the long grass and were creeping toward the center as it was cut.

At last the hrududu stopped and became silent. It had left a patch of long grass uncut, and this the men surrounded.

"Right, we'll go now," said El-ahrairah, and began to run as fast as he could away from the field, away from the farm and out into the open country beyond, with Rabscuttle hard on his heels. He did not want to hear the men shouting as they went forward, beating at the grass with their sticks. He did not want to see Burdock and his rabbits come scuttling out in all directions, to be clubbed and battered to death as they tried to get through the encircling men. One or two did get through, but the man with the gun did not miss them.

"Don't look back," said El-ahrairah to the trembling Rabscuttle, "and don't ever talk about it. We're going home—remember?—and something's telling me it's not very far now."

11

El-ahrairah and the Lendri

Tommy Brock . . . was not nice in his habits.
He ate wasp nests and frogs and worms: and he
waddled about by moonlight, digging things up.

BEATRIX POTTER, "The Tale of Mr. Tod"

Under conditions of tyranny it is far easier
to act than to think.

HANNAH ARENDT, quoted in W. H. AUDEN, *A Certain World*

For a few days (said Dandelion) after they had left poor Burdock and his rabbits, El-ahrairah and Rabscuttle traveled on uneventfully through the long-grass meadows and the summer weather.

One evening, as they were making themselves comfortable in the straw on the floor of an old barn, Rabscuttle said, "We're not far from home now, master. I can feel it all through my body, can't you?"

"Well, I can't feel it all through *your* body," replied El-ahrairah, who was often unable to resist gently teasing Rabscuttle, "but I can feel it, all right. All the same, I've got the notion that we may have to get past some big obstacle or

other before we get there. We'd better keep a good lookout
and go carefully. It would be a pity, wouldn't it, to stop running so close to home?"

It was getting late in the afternoon of the next day
when they came in sight of a thick forest. It was no ordinary
forest, as they could see. To right and left it stretched away
into the distance, and there seemed to be no gaps or open-
ings which might have been the beginnings of paths through
the tangle of trees and undergrowth.

"I'm afraid there's no help for it," said El-ahrairah,
when he had gazed at the forest and pondered for some
time. "Through that nasty-looking place we'll have to go. I
can tell that, can't you?"

"All too clearly, master, I'm afraid," answered Rabscuttle, sitting down in the grass and cleaning his face with his
front paws. "But we can't do it on our own. We're going to
need some kind of help. It would never do just to go plung-
ing into a place like that by ourselves. We'd be lost in half
an hour and dead in half a day."

"What sort of help, though?" asked El-ahrairah. "We'd
better start by trying to find someone who knows a bit more
about it than we do."

They had not gone far toward the forest before they
came upon a huge rat, almost as big as El-ahrairah himself.
It was sitting in the sun and no doubt, thought the rabbits,
meditating on the details of some vile and murderous
scheme. Neither of them liked the look of it at all, but all
the same, thought El-ahrairah, as the rat eyed him silently

with an evil and cunning expression, we've got to start somewhere. He greeted the rat politely and sat down beside it on the edge of a ditch.

"I wonder if you can give us some advice," he began. "We've got to get through that forest."

"What for?" asked the rat, its whiskers twitching unpleasantly.

"To get home," said El-ahrairah.

"Then how in bones and blazes do you come to be here?" asked the rat.

"It was on the orders of Lord Frith," answered El-ahrairah. "We had to undertake a long journey at his bidding. We're lucky to be alive. But now we're going home."

"You're not home yet," said the rat, showing its yellow teeth in an odious grin. "Not yet. Oh, no."

El-ahrairah made no reply, and for a little while there was silence.

"You'll never get through that forest," said the rat at length. "No one ever has, so far as I know."

"Do you know anyone who might help us, perhaps?" asked Rabscuttle.

"The only creature who might be able to help you, if he had a mind to it"—the rat sniggered—"would be Old Brock; but he'd be more likely to eat you than help you."

"Where can we find him?" asked El-ahrairah.

"He's not easily found," replied the rat. "He's always up and down along the edge of that forest, grubbing about. If you go up and down the edge too, he may find you. It's as good a way to be killed as any. Why should he help you? Have you thought of that?" It gave a sudden leap and was gone through the hedgerow.

It was getting on for ni-Frith on the following day before the two rabbits reached the outskirts of the forest. They were rough and wild, and to look further into it was not encouraging, to say the least. There seemed to be no big trees, which they took to mean that the trees were never thinned or cut back at all. The forest was an unkempt wilderness. The trees grew together so closely that even now, at midday, they shut out a great deal of the light. The undergrowth was thick; so thick that even the rabbits, accustomed to creeping through difficult places, could not see any way through it. They went further along the edge and looked again, but saw nothing better. El-ahrairah, who was persistent and not easily discouraged, continued looking along the outskirts for a long time, but at length was forced to admit himself at a loss.

"I suppose we'll have to try to find that Old Brock the rat talked about," he said to Rabscuttle.

"But if he's as likely to eat us as help us?" said Rabscuttle.

"He won't eat me in a hurry," replied El-ahrairah. "I tell you, I'm *determined* to get through that forest, and if it can only be done with the help of Old Brock, then I'm going to find him. And I've just had a thought. We're probably more likely to find him by night than by day, confound it."

Rabbits do not care to be about in darkness, which frightens them. Dawn and evening are their natural activity times. That night, even El-ahrairah felt a good deal of apprehension about setting out along the outskirts of the forest. The waning moon gave very little light, and every slight night sound, its source only to be guessed, was like an alarm. They made little progress and startled continually. However, they were lucky (if a swift outcome to a search of this kind could be called "lucky"). The night was not half gone when El-ahrairah, crouched at the foot of a tree and listening carefully, suddenly felt himself held down by a great paw, while a deep but very low voice said, "What are you doing here? Why are you here at all?"

El-ahrairah was half smothered and could not speak. It was greatly to Rabscuttle's credit that he did not run away but answered, "We are looking for—er—Lord Brock. Are you he, my lord?"

The huge badger made no move to release El-ahrairah as it said, "If I am, what does it matter to you? Why have you been looking for me?"

"We have to go through the forest, my lord—through it to the other side. It's our only way home. We've been told that nobody but you can help us."

At this, the badger raised its paw and allowed El-ahrairah to crawl out and sit up. It looked at the rabbits with a grim and hostile expression.

"Why do you suppose that I'll help you?"

"We have come a long way and overcome many

difficulties and dangers. We know you are the lord of this forest and can spare or kill whomever you choose. Pray, my lord, be patient while I tell you what we have undergone and how we come to be here."

And then, squatting in the waning moonlight at the feet of the lendri, El-ahrairah told it of King Darzin and the plight of his rabbits, of how Rabscuttle and he had confronted the Black Rabbit of Inlé, and of the dangers they had encountered in their journeyings since that time. "And we beg you, my lord," he ended, "to grant us your protection and help to overcome this last obstacle between ourselves and a peaceful homecoming. If there is any way in which we can help you or be of service to you, we'll gladly undertake it. You have only to command, and we'll do your bidding."

"I have a sett near here," growled the lendri. "You had better come with me."

They went with it as best they could along the tangled forest verge until they came to a kind of shallow pit, in one side of which was a great hole. In front of this lay a pile of earth mixed with withered grass and bracken. The lendri went down the hole, and the rabbits followed.

It was a daunting place: a maze of tunnels, leading in all directions and extending, so it seemed, over long distances. Indeed, the tunnels were so long that the rabbits became exhausted and had to beg the lendri to let them rest. But after a short time it became impatient and went on without a word, so that they were forced to stumble along behind it as best they could or else be left alone in the dark.

At last it stopped at a place which seemed no different from any other in the tunnels, except for being lined with straw and dried grass and for the overpowering stench of badger. The lendri lay down, waited for the rabbits to come up and then said, "How do you suppose that you can be of use to me?"

"We can forage for you, my lord," said El-ahrairah. "Tell us what you eat, and we'll find it and bring it to you."

"I eat everything. Chiefly worms; and beetles, cater-pillars, grubs, slugs and snails when they're to be found."

"We'll bring you plenty, my lord, if only you'll guide us through the forest when you're ready."

"Then you can start now."

It led them back aboveground to the forest verge. And now began surely the strangest life that rabbits can ever have led. Each night they met the lendri and foraged with it, sometimes in the forest, but usually in fields and even in the gardens of nearby houses. It was a long and tiring business, for the lendri was voracious and kept them at work until daybreak and sometimes after. It was horrible work for rab-bits. Often they dug in wet places for worms or, after rain, simply collected them aboveground. They carried them to the lendri in their mouths: not only worms but also slugs and snails and every small living creature they could find. Sometimes, although it was late in the season, they came upon pheasants' nests, and the lendri would crunch up the eggs with relish. Mice could often be caught, since by in-stinct they were not afraid of rabbits. At first the rabbits were nauseated by mouthing worms and slugs, but as they grew used to it, they ceased to be troubled at all.

Harder to bear was the dislike and contempt they incurred among their fellow creatures. As they became known in the fields and copses, they came to be universally hated and despised. For several nights, from tree to tree, a squirrel followed them, chattering, "Slaves! Lendri's slaves! Work harder or Master will be angry." On another night a wounded and helpless rat sneered, "I'm delighted to be of use to the cowardly rabbits." Owls gave warning of their approach, and voles squeaked insults from the safety of their holes. It was as depressing and unnatural a life as could be for rabbits, by nature gregarious and the least carnivorous of creatures. They grew surly and short-tempered with each other and often felt on the point of giving up the disgusting work and running away. And yet they knew the lendri was their only hope of getting home.

At the outset they had supposed that as they got to know the lendri it would treat them in a more friendly way. However, it did not. Its manner to them remained bleak and cold. It seldom spoke except to give orders or warnings of danger, or to find fault with something they had done. It never commended their work. Initially El-ahrairah did his best to converse with it, but was met only with silence or inattention. They grew less alert, less swift, less responsive to the countless signals that healthy rabbits continually receive from the wind, from scents and from noises and movement round about them.

One cold, wet morning, when they both felt worn out by a long night of carrying worms, Rabscuttle said, "Master, do you think we could get the lendri to say *when* it will release us and take us through the forest? For I don't know how much more of this I can stand; and you don't look or smell right either, for the matter of that."

El-ahrairah plucked up courage to ask the lendri that night, but the only reply he got was: "When I'm ready. Work harder and I may feel like it."

One night they met a hare in the fields. After the usual scornful and wounding words, it ended, "And why you're doing it I can't imagine and nor can anyone else." El-ahrairah explained why they were doing it. "And do you seriously suppose that that lendri will ever let you go and help you on your way?" asked the hare. "Of course it won't. It'll simply keep you working until you either die or run away."

At this, even El-ahrairah felt close to despair. Yet had he only known it, Lord Frith was not so far away from his faithful rabbits as they thought.

Two or three nights later, as they were digging for worms quite near the sett, Rabscuttle noticed a place where the ground had been newly disturbed. "Look, master," he said. "Look at all that loose earth. That's not been dug long. It wasn't like that the other day. It'll be a good place for worms, don't you think?"

They began digging in the soft soil. They had not dug very deep before El-ahrairah paused, sniffing and hesitating. "Come over here, Rabscuttle, and tell me what you think."

Rabscuttle also sniffed. "There's something been buried, master, not so long ago. Something that's been alive but isn't now. Should we let it alone?"

"No," replied El-ahrairah. "We'll go on."

They dug deeper. "Master, that's a hand, the hand of a human being."

"Yes," said El-ahrairah. "The hand of a woman. And if I'm not mistaken, the whole body's there. It wouldn't smell like that otherwise."

"Surely we'd better leave it, master?"

"No," said El-ahrairah. "We'll uncover some more."

In the darkness and silence, they went on digging until it was plain that a whole human body had been buried.

"Now just leave a light covering of earth," said El-ahrairah, "and we'll go away and forage somewhere else. What we want is for human beings to find that body, and soon."

It was two days, however, before a man, wearing heavy boots and carrying a gun, came strolling along the verge of the forest. The rabbits, watching from the mouth of the sett, saw him catch sight of the newly dug ground, stop to look more closely, then go up to it and kick away some of the earth. As soon as he was sure of what was there, he marked the place with a torn-off branch and set off running as best he could with his gun and clumsy boots.

"Now we'll go and tell the lendri," said El-ahrairah.

Having heard what they had to tell him, the lendri joined them near the mouth of the sett. They had not long to wait. A hrududu, full of men, drove up and stopped nearby. The men got out and began surrounding the place where the body lay, with posts which had blue-and-white tape running between them. More men came, until there seemed to be men everywhere, talking together in loud voices.

The lendri, plainly very much afraid, turned and went back down the tunnel as fast as it could. The two rabbits followed it.

"We *must* keep up with it," panted El-ahrairah, "wherever it goes."

Scrambling and stumbling, they followed the lendri down a side tunnel where they had never been before. It seemed not to have been used for some time past. In places it was partly blocked by fallen earth, which the lendri flung aside or behind it with great strokes of its paws. The rabbits were showered with earth and sometimes struck painfully by small stones, but still struggled on behind the terrified lendri, which was clearly intent upon nothing but getting away from the men.

After what seemed a long time, the tunnel led slowly upward and came out in the open air. At the mouth the lendri stopped, sniffing, listening and looking all about. Finally it came cautiously out into the forest, went a short distance forward and concealed itself in the cover of some thick bushes.

"I don't think it knew we were following," whispered El-ahrairah. "We'll wait now until it moves off."

As they waited, they listened for the sound of the men, but could hear only the faintest noise in the distance. "We must have come quite a long way," whispered El-ahrairah. "Creep out now, as quietly as you can. We can't stay here. If anything frightens the lendri, it'll bolt back into this hole and trample us down."

They managed to slink silently some way along the forest floor, stopping at length as they came to a small clearing. Making his way cautiously round its edge, El-ahrairah found what he was looking for—the marks of tires in the muddy ground. They led away down a slight descent, and the rabbits followed them until they heard men talking nearby and smelled white sticks. They waited a long time in the undergrowth, until at last the men started up their hrududu and drove away.

The sound receded in the distance. "Come on," said El-ahrairah. "We need to get out while it's still light."

They had not gone far before they found themselves on the edge of the forest and looking out at green fields.

"But is this edge the one we want, master?" asked Rabscuttle. "I mean, it could be another part of the edge where we were, couldn't it?"

"Look at the sun," replied El-ahrairah. "It's almost in our eyes. The breeze is coming from in front of us too. This is the sunset side of the forest, all right."

And so it proved. They slept that night in a thick bramble bush. Nothing disturbed them, and the following afternoon they came back to their own warren.

"So the Black Rabbit was as good as his word," said El-ahrairah, gazing about him. "Not an enemy to be smelled, a fine evening, and everyone at silflay. They look all right too. Well done, Rabscuttle."

"Well done, master," replied Rabscuttle, touching his nose to El-ahrairah's. "Look, here's a patch of clover. Let's sit down and eat it before we do anything else."

However, as has been recounted elsewhere, their home-coming was by no means all that they could have wished.

PART III

12

The Secret River

The name of the second river is Gihon. No sooner has it
come out of Paradise than it vanishes beneath the depths of
the sea . . . whence, through secret passages of the earth
it emerges again in the mountains of Ethiopia.

MOSES BAR CEPHA, quoted by JOHN L. LOWES
in *The Road to Xanadu*

Of the does who had escaped with him from Efrafa,
Vilthuril always seemed to Bigwig the most strange and
enigmatic, the hardest to understand. Not that she was unfriendly or standoffish. On the contrary, she was on good
terms with every rabbit in the warren and was often ready
enough for a chat: about such things as the weather, the
grass, and the horses which galloped on the Down—about
anything, really, which could give rise to no disagreement
and upon which anyone could express a harmless view. She
was a good mother and devoted to her mate, Fiver. She and
Fiver had, in fact, discovered their affinity almost before the
return from the Efrafan expedition: and during the night of
Woundwort's attack—which, it will be recalled, Fiver had

spent lying unconscious among Efrafans on the floor of the Honeycomb before awakening to defeat Vervain without striking a blow—Vilthuril had been distracted and almost mad with anxiety on his account.

In dealings with Vilthuril, everyone sensed a certain reserve on her part and knew that she and Fiver spent much time in their inward world, the world of the mystic. No one resented this, since they instinctively recognized its validity, and anyway, as Bluebell remarked, so long as Fiver could emerge from it for the short time he required to demolish rabbits like Vervain, it seemed all to the good.

Not that Vilthuril could not speak seriously and command the respect and attention of others when she wanted to; and since she did not want to very often, other rabbits usually piped down simply not to miss the opportunity of getting a bit of the real Vilthuril while it was going. This they seldom or never regretted.

One evening, in quite a full Honeycomb and certainly to his surprise, she remarked quietly to Hazel, almost as though they were alone together, "Has Hyzenthlay ever told you about the underground river in Efrafa?"

"The *what*?" replied Hazel, startled for once out of his self-possession.

"The underground river in Efrafa," repeated Vilthuril in the same quiet, conversational tone.

"No, she certainly hasn't," said Hazel. And then, more to keep himself in countenance than for any other reason, he asked, "Bigwig, have *you* ever heard of the underground river in Efrafa? After all, you've been there and I haven't."

"No, I'll be snared if I have," answered Bigwig, "and what's more, I'd need a lot of persuading that there was one at all."

"There was," said Vilthuril, "but only three of us knew of its existence."

"Hyzenthlay?" asked Hazel. "Did you know about it?"

"Oh, yes," said Hyzenthlay. "Thethuthinnang and I, we both knew the river well. The *secret* river, we used to call it. Do go on, Vilthuril. Tell them about the secret river. She was closest to it. She found it first and knew more about it than we did," she added to Hazel and Bigwig. "It was a matter of being, well, attuned to it more than anything else."

There was a pause, as though Vilthuril was collecting herself to begin.

At length she said, "It's almost impossible to convey to anyone who wasn't there what it was like to be a rabbit in Efrafa. In the burrows, between a Mark's two silflays of the day, you weren't really alive—not in the sense that everyone here understands it. The officers—whenever one of them happened to come into one of the Mark burrows—didn't actually stop you moving about. But there wasn't much point in moving about. In the first place it was usually rather difficult, because the burrows were crowded, but also one place in a burrow was much the same as anywhere else. It was the same with talking: you were forbidden to talk, but as a rule there wasn't much to talk about. I always felt that the officers wanted you to do absolutely nothing: to keep still, not to talk and not even to think, between silflays, unless you were required for mating, and there wasn't much enjoyment in that. A rabbit who wasn't there can't really understand what the life was like.

"Now, one day—or it may have been one night, for all I knew—I was sleeping or half sleeping—drowsing—at the furthest end of one of the Mark burrows—that's to say, the furthest away from the run leading up and out—when I began to sense something odd; something I'd never come across before. A current was coming through the burrow wall. It wasn't a current of water or a current of air. It wasn't warm and it wasn't cold either. But something was coming through the wall and flowing away down the burrow; not spreading out into a pool and flooding it, as you might expect, but flowing down the length of it in a channel of its own.

"By moving a little I was able to lie directly in its path—whatever it was—and then to face it head-on. And now there could be no doubt about it at all. A stream of something was coming through the burrow wall and breaking over me before it flowed away. It was slow but quite steady. No other rabbit in the burrow seemed to be in the least aware of it.

"I lay there a long time, giving myself entirely up to it; letting it take possession of me, you might say. And eventually I came to grasp that what was coming to me through the wall was a flow of *knowledge*: knowledge that wasn't mine and had nothing to do with me. It wasn't my own imagination playing tricks. It wasn't a fancy originating in my own head. This was something from outside—outside

Efrafa—that I was receiving. You couldn't drink it or smell it or feel it on your fur as hot or cold. But you could move out of it and get back into it again. I did this several times, to be sure.

"It was trying to convey something, either to me or else to any other rabbit that might be able to receive it. I lay in it and tried to make my own mind as empty as I could. And sure enough, an idea came in quite clearly: an idea of two rabbits—two adult female rabbits—alone together, somewhere far from Efrafa. And as soon as I had grasped this, the stream made the knowledge larger. These were two does who had left their own warren in order to start a new one: a warren in which the does would predominate, a warren ruled by does.

"There could be no question of this being an idea starting in my own head. I didn't have any sort of picture in my imagination. I simply knew of the two does' existence and of what they meant to do. I couldn't see them at all in my mind's eye, but I knew their names—Flyairth and Prake—and I knew they were somewhere out there, so strong and confident about what they meant to do that they could persuade other rabbits, bucks and does, to come with them. But where? All I could know was that it was somewhere sandy, on a gentle slope.

"I must have stayed a long time in the flow of that underground river, because when I finally came out I felt exhausted. I fell sound asleep and slept until the Mark's next silflay, which was in the early afternoon. I wanted to talk to someone, to tell them about what I'd found—or about what had found me. But it was always dangerous to talk to anyone in Efrafa. Either they might be a Council spy or else—which was more likely—they might pass on what you'd told them, until everybody knew it as gossip.

"I decided to tell Hyzenthlay, who I knew had got on the wrong side of the Council for asking to be allowed to leave Efrafa. I told her during silflay that afternoon, and she said she'd come down with me and find out whether she could feel the current in the way I had.

"She came, and she felt it, though not as strongly as I had, or so it seemed to me. But anyway, now there were two of us, and of course we were wondering whether other rabbits would discover it for themselves. We felt frightened of what might happen to us if the officers got to know. We hadn't done anything wrong, but believe me, that wasn't enough to keep you out of trouble in Efrafa. We were afraid we might be killed, because the Council would want to stop anyone else discovering the river. Or else they'd say that we'd made it all up. And of course Hyzenthlay was under the Council's suspicion already. So we didn't tell anyone else.

"What came to me down the secret river that night was the knowledge that Flyairth and Prake had persuaded a whole lot of rabbits—bucks as well as does—to leave their warren and come to the sandy place where they meant to start a new one of their own. Just that I came to know and nothing more. But that night Hyzenthlay came to know it too, without asking me. So we both felt sure that it was true.

"The next afternoon both Hyzenthlay and I were among the last coming down from silflay, and we found Thethuthinnang in my usual place at the far end of the burrow. We both felt fairly sure we could trust her with our secret, but we waited so see whether she'd find it by herself. It was soon clear to us that she was aware of something strange and puzzling, but we left it at that until silflay the next day, when we told her what we'd come to know ourselves. She'd felt it too, but less clearly than I had, and she hadn't been able to understand that it was a flow of knowledge until we told her.

"After that, we all did our best to get into the secret river at least once a day or night. As a rule, the other two didn't receive the knowledge as clearly as I did, but after we'd been able to talk about it together, they always realized what had been coming on the current while they were in it.

"After some time, we all three began to feel that we knew Flyairth and Prake well. But there were two things we didn't know. We didn't know whether those two does had anything to do with sending us this knowledge; and we didn't know whether the flow was going anywhere else besides Efrafa—to any other warren, I mean, or to any other rabbits. You see, we could do nothing to reply. All we could do was to receive the knowledge coming down the secret river, and to agree together, every day, about what it had been.

"We all knew that Flyairth and Prake had established their warren—Thinial, they called it—as they wanted it, and that the bucks seemed content under the control of the does. Bucks who discovered that they didn't like it after all simply left, and no one stopped them. The small Owsla of does were well liked. They were certainly the cleverest rabbits to be found and didn't bully others into resentment.

"Several of them, so it seemed, bore litters of their own. They chose bucks whom they liked and mated with them. Then later, when they came to bear their young, they stood down from the Owsla for as long as they needed to bring them up and train them to look after themselves. When the young rabbits didn't need them anymore, they rejoined the Owsla.

"Flyairth had two litters in this way, and as far as we could learn, her young rabbits had turned out well.

"We received nothing else for a long time, and I supposed that now that Thinial was established and flourishing, there was nothing more for us to learn and the secret river knowledge had come to a natural end. I can't say I was sorry. The whole business frightened me. I was always afraid that somehow or other, General Woundwort would get to know. And yet I kept on, every night, lying in the river. It fascinated me: I couldn't keep out of it.

"And then, one night, I found myself caught up in a kind of violent mist of confusion and turmoil out of which, for a long time, nothing came; or nothing I could understand, anyway. The others were as lost in it as I.

"At last one thing stood out clearly—that is, one piece of knowledge. And that was the White Blindness. None of us had ever seen a rabbit dying of the White Blindness, but we knew as much as is common knowledge to all rabbits: how an infected rabbit stumbles about in the open, seeing nothing, so that in the end it may stagger into water and drown. And how other rabbits often become infected, so that a whole warren may be destroyed. We knew that it takes a rabbit a long time to die of the White Blindness.

"All three of us received, that night, knowledge of the Blindness. It didn't do anything; it was simply there, like a stone or a tree. We didn't think it was coming down the secret river to infect us, but the mere knowledge of it, dominating everything else in the river and turning it into incomprehensible turbulence, was frightening enough.

"Two nights later, the knowledge grew wider. Flyairth, wandering by herself outside Thinial, had come upon a solitary rabbit, a hlessi, lurching about and dying of the Blindness. Horrified, she kept away from it, but then she saw that it was approaching Thinial of its own accord. Yet at the last moment, apparently, it crawled away in another direction.

"That was all that the river brought us that night.

"For several nights afterward, we learned of nothing but Flyairth's growing obsession with the Blindness. She knew that if in some way or other it got into Thinial, it would destroy it.

"It wasn't I," said Vilthuril, "it was Hyzenthlay who came to know from the river that Flyairth meant to go to any lengths to keep the Blindness out of Thinial. Her great fear was that an infected rabbit—some stranger—might wander into the warren. One strange thing about the Blindness, as I expect you all know, is that infected rabbits are able to mate and quite often do.

"Flyairth told her Owsla of her fear, and they agreed

that everything possible must be done to keep infected rabbits out of the warren. By day, all strangers were refused entry, whether or not they could be seen or smelled to be ill. By night, the task was more difficult. A stranger could get in unseen. The bucks agreed to take it in turns to keep a night watch—four bucks each night—to guard against strangers.

"That was all we learned for many days. And then the knowledge reached us that an infected buck, a stranger, had got into Thinial by night and mated with one of the does, who had become pregnant. One of the bucks who had been on watch admitted that he had fought the stranger, who had beaten him and then entered the warren. Understandably, perhaps, he had said nothing and hoped that he'd hear no more of the matter. The pregnant doe, Milmown, had no buck of her own, and told the Owsla that the stranger had mated with her and then gone his way.

"All might yet have been well, if Milmown had not developed the Blindness. When it was plain that she had, Flyairth and Prake were implacable. Milmown, though pitied by many, was driven out of Thinial by the Owsla and told never to return.

"But she didn't go away. She remained a short distance from the warren and constantly pleaded, to anyone who would listen, to be allowed to return. And for some reason the progress of the disease in her was delayed. She scratched a hole in the sand and there she bore her litter: no more than four rabbits, blind, deaf and furless. When they had become old enough to fend for themselves, the White Blindness once more continued to run its course, and Milmown died.

"And now all that the three of us could learn from the secret river was the same knowledge, repeated day after day. We knew that the four young rabbits of Milmown's litter were living as best they could in the open, not far from Thinial, and that although they didn't appear to have the Blindness, the Chief Rabbit refused to give them help or shelter. No one could say she was wrong, but few would themselves have felt able to enforce such severity.

"I think many in Thinial must have expected the young rabbits to fall victim to the Thousand, but no elil appeared, and we learned from the secret river that they continued to survive.

"Then we began to receive fresh knowledge, something that hadn't come down the river before. At first it was confused and fragmentary, and we couldn't make anything of it at all, until Thethuthinnang said that she thought it had something to do with rabbits in Thinial becoming opposed to Flyairth. Once we'd grasped that, the knowledge began to reach us more clearly. The root of it was that Milmown had been well liked in the warren and had had a good many friends, including two or three of the Owsla. These friends hadn't been able to do anything for her when she had been driven out, because she had the Blindness; she would die, and that was all there was to it. But now that she was dead and her four young, as far as anyone could see, had not got the Blindness, a number of her former friends began saying that Flyairth and Prake were going too far and that to leave Milmown's young to die outside the warren was going to unnecessary and cruel lengths. Flyairth, however, refused to consider any change. For her, the safety and survival of Thinial were all-important and justified any severity.

"However, more and more rabbits began to drift away from her. They could see with their own eyes the young rabbits who had been abandoned, but they couldn't envisage an epidemic of the White Blindness which was not there. Some began going out to meet and talk to Milmown's youngsters, telling them that they personally would like to see them brought into the warren; and to put a stop to this sort of thing was very difficult for the Owsla.

"And then the river knowledge came to me, hard-breathing in the crowded Near Hind burrow one hot summer night, that several rabbits had come together, brought Milmown's young into Thinial and given them an empty burrow of their own, in defiance of the Owsla. When Flyairth herself came to order them to leave, she was met by does from among those who had come with her to found the warren, who said that the young rabbits were not to be evicted. Flyairth, a heavy, tough doe, fought and beat two or three of them. But she could not fight them all.

"For many days the river brought us nothing more. All the knowledge we received was of the helpless anger of Flyairth, as she went among one group of her rabbits after another, doing all she could to assert her authority. We—the three of us in Efrafa—thought that she would have done better to let the matter drop. But she was so much obsessed by her fear of the Blindness that she couldn't weigh up its probability or improbability. As long as there was the least chance of it reentering Thinial, she must take every possible step to prevent it. And night upon night the secret river brought us nothing but the knowledge of her ceaseless anger and determination.

"I shall never forget lying, sometimes half the night, against the burrow wall in Efrafa, conscious of nothing but Flyairth's rage pouring over me and wondering how it could be that others could not feel it. It was by far the strongest and most powerful flood of knowledge we had yet received.

"Flyairth's position as Chief Rabbit was very much weakened by the whole business of Milmown's young, especially because she had refused to give way.

"It was just at this time that she bore her third litter. She was obliged to relinquish her position as Chief Rabbit to look after them, and of course this restricted her and diminished her influence in the warren.

"There were rabbits who said that since she still refused to give way over Milmown's young, she had better cease to be Chief Rabbit.

"And it was just at this point that we lost the chance of gaining any more knowledge of Thinial or of Flyairth and her desperation. But it wasn't anything to do with the secret river. It was because Bigwig was brought into Efrafa and made an officer in the Near Hind Mark—our Mark. When did you first talk to Hyzenthlay about the escape, Bigwig?"

"It was the night of the same day that I joined the Mark," replied Bigwig. "In my burrow, Hyzenthlay. Do you remember? The plan was that you'd pick the does for the escape. Then you'd tell them that same day and we'd break out that evening. The less time they had to think about it, the better."

"But we couldn't do it that evening, because Woundwort kept you talking."

"So we had to make it the next evening—the evening of the thunderstorm. The evening they arrested Nelthilta."

"How many nights did you actually spend in Efrafa, then?" asked Vilthuril.

"Three."

"I remember," said Hyzenthlay. "I was terrified at the idea of all those does knowing about the escape for a whole night and a day. I thought we were bound to be discovered. I was right too. If Nelthilta had been arrested a little earlier, that would have been that."

"My last night in Efrafa," said Vilthuril, "was the night we all spent knowing about the plan and having to wait. And that was the last night, too, that I went into the secret river. I was the only one of the three of us."

"I had no heart for it that night," said Hyzenthlay. "Thethuthinnang and I were both worried to death that the plan would be discovered."

"That night," said Vilthuril, "I learned nothing—nothing more than I already knew about the growing opposition to Flyairth. I wonder how it all turned out."

"The strangest thing of all, to me," said Hyzenthlay, "is that we haven't the least idea where Thinial is or where those rabbits are. They might be many days' journey away, or they might be quite near us."

"It's the strangest story I've ever heard," said Hazel.

It was not the underground "river" which seemed incredible to Hazel and the other rabbits who had listened to Vilthuril's story. When meeting with phenomena, none of them ever thought in terms of a division between what was credible and what was not. The idea of the inexplicable meant nothing to them; they did not need it. So much that was inexplicable—for example, the phases of the moon—lay around them that they simply accepted it as part of their lives. True, the "river" lay outside their own experience, but so did much else. What struck them as extraordinary was that Vilthuril should have received this story—this information—never mind how, about rabbits distant from themselves, rabbits not one of whom they had ever seen. As she told it, these far-off rabbits had not communicated to her the knowledge she had received: it had simply come to her, almost as though she had been in Thinial herself. If it had not reached her by way of an underground river—and no doubt there were plenty of them in the world—then it would have come in some other way. Why? Well, said some, it must have been drifting about, to be almost accidentally picked up by rabbits like Fiver and Vilthuril; and that was strange. Not altogether, said others. It was common knowledge that Fiver and Vilthuril possessed unusual sensibilities.

There was no general agreement, and it was left to Blackberry to reach a conclusion which anyone could comfortably accept. "I doubt whether we've heard the last of it."

13

The New Warren

A Cold Coming they had of it: . . . just, the worst time
of the year, to take a journey . . . the weather sharp,
the days short, the sun farthest off.

BISHOP LANCELOT ANDREWES, Sermon 15:
"Of the Nativity"

Kehaar, the black-headed gull, was flying westward above the land between Caesar's Belt and the Down. He flew low and in irregular curves from north to south and back, alighting every now and then at his leisure to feed for a while across any piece of likely-looking ground which attracted him.

He was not in the best of tempers. Naturally aggressive and quick to annoyance, like most gulls who live in competition with a myriad of others, he did not always like being asked to carry out tasks by the Watership Down rabbits. Showing pugnacity and attacking their enemies was one thing. Searching was another. Five months before, he had enjoyed taking part in their conflict with Efrafa, in diving on the formidable General Woundwort, in covering the retreat of Bigwig and the fugitive does in their flight from Efrafa and helping them to escape down the river. What he liked was onslaught. Nevertheless, after the rabbits had saved his life while he was lying injured and helpless on the Down, he had willingly performed for them the reconnaissance which had so unluckily ended in nothing better than his discovery of Efrafa.

Now, to have been asked to carry out another, similar flight had annoyed him, though not to the extent of refusing to do it. It had been tactfully requested. Hazel, who knew very well that of all his rabbits Bigwig was Kehaar's particular admirer and friend, had shrewdly left to him the business of explaining to the gull their purpose and what they wanted him to look for.

"We're going to start a new warren, Kehaar," Bigwig had said, dodging here and there between the gull's orange-colored legs as he strutted over the thinning November grass, "before this one gets crowded out. Half the rabbits will come from here and half from Efrafa. We want you to find us the right place and then go to Efrafa and ask Captain Campion to come and meet us there and have a look at it."

"Vat kind of place you vant?" replied Kehaar. "And vhere do you vant it?"

"Somewhere out there on the sunset side," said Bigwig, "about halfway between here and Efrafa. It mustn't be anywhere near men's houses or gardens: that's very important. And we need a dry place, where digging's going to be easy. What would be perfect would be a bank on the edge of a copse where men don't come much and there are a few bushes to conceal the holes."

"I find him," answered Kehaar shortly. "Den I come and tell you, show you vhere. Show Efrafa fellow vhere too, yes?"

"That'll be grand, Kehaar. Splendid bird! What a friend you've been to us! We couldn't possibly do it without you."

"Not for vait about. I go now. Come back tomorrow, you come 'ere for me tell you, yes?"

"I'll be here. Mind out for the cats, won't you?"

"*Yark!* Damn' cat: 'e no catch me again."

With this he took off, flying southward in the chilly sunshine.

He flew over Hare Warren Farm and down to the strip of woodland known as Caesar's Belt. Here he foraged for a time and exchanged chat with a few gulls like himself.

"There's bad weather on the way," said one of these. "Very bad weather; the worst we've ever known. Snow and bitter cold out of the west. If you don't want to die, Kehaar, you'd better find some shelter."

Kehaar, flying on westward, soon felt, in the mysterious and unaccountable way of his kind, the impending cold which the chance-met gull had warned him of. Muttering "Damn' rabbits no fly," he went as far as Beacon Hill before turning back along a line further to the north. Soon he came upon as perfect a site for a warren as any rabbit could well wish for: a lonely, shallow bank facing southwest on the edge of a wood of ash and silver birch. In front lay a grassy field, where three or four horses were grazing.

He alighted and looked about him. Clearly, men must come fairly often to see to the horses, but equally clearly there was no likelihood of the meadow being plowed. He could see no sign of possession by rabbits—no holes, no hraka. He would be unlikely to find a better place. It lay, he judged, rather nearer Efrafa than Watership, but this was nothing against it in the light of its obvious merits.

The following day he met Bigwig, together with Hazel, Groundsel and Thethuthinnang, and told them of his discovery. Hazel, after praising him warmly, asked him to go to Efrafa, tell Campion, and find out how soon he could join them for a meeting at the site itself.

The business of arranging a meeting involved complications and a certain amount of danger. Campion would need to be guided by Kehaar, already surly at being asked to do so much. But the Watership rabbits would also need guiding. Plainly, one party would have to wait on the site for the others to arrive. There would be danger from elil. It was some time before everything was fixed. Campion sent word that he would start as soon as he learned from Kehaar that Hazel and the others had already reached the bank and were waiting for him. This would mean that the Watership rabbits would have to spend at least a night and a day in the open.

"Well, there's no help for it," said Hazel, "and at least we'll have Kehaar with us for the night, to attack any elil that may turn up. I'm ready to start tomorrow, if we can get there in a day."

"Ya, you get dere in a day," said Kehaar. "I take you, den next day fly to Efrafa, bring Meester Campion before dark."

They arrived at the site in early evening, and after sil-flay in the meadow, settled down to sleep in the long grass.

In the half darkness of the moonlit night they were attacked by a male stoat. It was plainly confident of making an easy kill, but it had reckoned without Kehaar. Alerted by the frantic squealing of the rabbits, the gull dived from the ash tree where he had settled for the night, and wounded the stoat severely before it was able to extricate itself and make off into the copse. "I no kill 'im," said Kehaar ruefully, in reply to the rabbits' thanks, "but all the same 'e get big surprise, 'e no come back."

The following morning Groundsel consulted with Hazel and Bigwig. "I'm not easily frightened by elil," he said. "Woundwort knew that: that was why he picked me for his attack on your warren. But I don't fancy living in a place that's crawling with stoats and weasels."

"You'll be all right once your holes are dug," said Bigwig. "What do you think, Hazel-rah? Ought they to start digging, at once, perhaps?"

At this point they were joined by Kehaar, who had evidently overheard Bigwig.

"You no start holes now," he said to Hazel as though giving an order. "You take your rabbits home plenty damn' quick."

"But why, Kehaar?" asked Hazel. "I thought we were

all ready now to bring out rabbits from both warrens and get started."

"You no get started now," said the gull, even more emphatically. "You start now, you lose every damn' rabbit you got."

"But how?"

"Cold. Frost, snow, ice, every damn' t'ing. Coming soon, very bad."

"Are you sure?"

"*Yark!* Ask any bird you like. Any rabbit try to stay 'ere, live in open, 'e frozen dead. Vinter cold coming, Meester 'Azel: bad, bad cold. You take rabbits home, whole damn' lot today."

"But you brought us here yesterday and never said anything about frost."

"I no feel 'im yesterday. Yesterday I t'ink you got time to start. But today feel different. You no got time. Cold coming very soon."

Knowing and trusting Kehaar as they did, the four Watership rabbits set off for home at once, while the gull flew to Efrafa to tell Campion that the project was postponed. Campion was skeptical. "It doesn't look like frost to me."

"Den you go out dere, you make damn' fine ice rabbit," said Kehaar, and flew away without another word.

14

Flyairth

Just as the gull had said, the unexpected cold was not long in coming. During the very night after their return, there was a sharp frost. The cold continued throughout the following day, and next night the frost was even more bitter. It was clear to all Hazel's rabbits that now they were in for the winter cold of which Kehaar had warned them. From then on, keen frosts lasted all day and each night were intensified under empty, clear skies. From horizon to horizon the stars glittered with an icy brilliance, and below them nothing moved on the frozen ground. Birds and animals either starved or else left the Down to try their luck below, in the fields and gardens of Ecchinswell or Kingsclere. The owls and kestrels perforce followed their prey, and from Beacon Hill to Cottington's Clump the high ridges were deserted.

None of Hazel's rabbits had ever experienced so prolonged or bitter a frost. There was little nourishment in the thin, many-times-nibbled grass, and little warmth to be gained from bodies huddled together underground. They became torpid and drowsy. Some supposed that the frost would never come to an end, and were hard to convince that endurance was worthwhile and their proper response, as ordained by Lord Frith.

One afternoon the cold lessened slightly. Cloud filled the western sky and moved gradually closer until it lay overhead. Heavy it seemed, as though carrying an invisible load pressing upon the Down and holding it even stiller than the frost. There was not the least wind, yet the cloud mass, which now filled the whole sky, moved slowly eastward, thickening as it came.

Snow began to fall; at first only a little, scattered here and there and gone as it reached the ground. A light but bitter breeze sprang up, driving the flakes before it as they increased. Soon the fall grew heavy, so that there was nothing to be seen through the flakes but more distant flakes, spinning and whirling as they fell. Before long they began to cover the grass, lying between the tussocks in patches which grew and came together to form sheets. By dusk the whole Down was overlaid, and onto the smooth whiteness fell more snow, slowly covering and deepening the fragile mass.

Gazing out at the snow, Hazel, who had done his best

every day to meet and talk with all his rabbits, knew that the time had come to lead them down to the winter burrows dug by Bluebell, Pipkin and the does during the autumn. He had never been to look them over, and for this he blamed himself. One thing was sure: there could be no more digging now, with the ground hard as rock. They would have to take the winter burrows as they found them.

However, he thought that first he would go down the hill by himself and see what the burrows were like. Then he realized that he would have to take Bluebell with him, since Bluebell had assured him that the holes were well concealed, and without him he would probably not be able to find them. Finally he decided to take Bluebell, Pipkin and any of the does who wanted to come.

He had got them together and was on the point of setting out, when he was joined by Bigwig, who wondered where they were going and why. When Hazel told him, he asked to join the party, and Hazel, peering out into the still-falling snow, felt glad enough to take him along.

The snow caused them no difficulty over the direction to take, for it was simply a matter of running the short distance to the northern edge of the Down and then descending the steep slope to its foot. They could see almost nothing, however, through the falling snow, and neither Bluebell nor Pipkin could remember where the holes were and how far along the foot of the Down they needed to go. After some fruitless searching, Pipkin ventured to say that he thought they had come too far and ought to turn back and look along a particular bank which he now recalled.

He was proved right almost at once, when Bluebell, going a little way up a snowy slope, came upon one of the holes, concealed by a clump of thistles.

Hazel and Bigwig found him crouching over the mouth of the hole, looking at it in an uncertain way, as though puzzled.

"Hazel-rah," he said, "if I'm not mistaken, this hole's been in use for quite some time. What's more, I think there are some rabbits down there now." He moved aside. "See what you think."

Hazel put his front paws through the snow. He could not be sure, but certainly he seemed to feel a scraped depression in the frozen ground and a slight irregularity in the mouth of the hole itself. There was a fresh smell of rabbits. He turned to Bigwig.

"I think he's right. There *are* some rabbits down there. We'd better go in ourselves, I suppose, and find out who they are."

So saying, without hesitation he went into the hole. He knew that Bigwig was behind him and felt sure enough that the others would follow. It was quite a long run, without obstructions, but as far as he could tell there was no enemy waiting for him at the other end. He came out into the burrow and paused for Bigwig to join him.

It was at this moment that he found himself confronted by a heavy, burly doe, a complete stranger. Her manner was hostile, and behind her was clustered a group of several younger rabbits.

"What do you think you're doing, coming in here?" said the doe. "Get out, before I—"

She stopped on seeing Bigwig behind Hazel, and as she hesitated Bluebell and Pipkin came out into the burrow, followed by four does.

"I think *you'd* better tell *us* who you are and what you're doing here," said Hazel, quietly but firmly. "This is our burrow. We dug it."

As the doe still hesitated, Bigwig, at Hazel's side, said tentatively, "Could you possibly be . . . are you . . . that is . . . is your name Flyairth, and have you come from Thinial?"

At this, the doe started, trembling with real fear. Her whole manner changed. Bigwig said nothing more. At length she replied, "Who are you? How could you know—" She broke off.

In a tone of greater confidence, Bigwig repeated, "Is your name Flyairth?"

"Have *you* come from Thinial, then?" she asked him.

"No, I haven't," answered Bigwig. "For the third time, is your name Flyairth?"

Hazel interposed. "Let's all settle down comfortably and explain ourselves to one another." Sitting down himself, he went on: "The burrows where we usually live are higher up, not far from here. We dug these burrows down here last autumn, to have somewhere more sheltered to go when it started snowing. We don't want to quarrel with you, but naturally we were surprised to find you here."

The doe spoke to Bigwig. "How do you know my name and where I've come from?"

"I can't explain," replied Bigwig, "or not now, anyway. Whether or not you can stay is for our Chief Rabbit here to decide."

Still she persisted. "But have you been to Thinial? How do you know about Thinial?"

"Never mind about that now," said Hazel. "We just want you to know that we're not your enemies. You can stay—for the time being. Bigwig here and I are going back up the hill now to bring down the rest of our rabbits."

"Let me come with you," said the doe. "I've never been up the hill as yet, and I ought to get to know your warren as soon as I can."

"All right," said Hazel, "but we shan't be able to show you much tonight. I just want to get our rabbits down here as quick as we can and let them settle in and go to sleep."

"I won't be any trouble to you," said Flyairth. "There's a full moon, so I'll be able to tag along quite easily."

"It's no distance, anyway," said Hazel. "We shan't be long. Bluebell and Hlao-roo, and you does—will you stay here until we come back? If the other two burrows are as good as this one, Bluebell, there'll be quite enough room for all of us."

"They're expandable, Hazel-rah, you see," said Bluebell. "The more rabbits you put in them, the bigger they get. And warmer too."

When Hazel, together with Bigwig and Flyairth, left the hole, night had fallen. The cloud had broken up, and the full moon, shining on the snow, gave them plenty of light. As they came off the steep slope and onto the top of the Down, Bigwig stopped, sniffing the air and looking about him.

"Wait a moment, Hazel-rah. There's something—well, something unusual."

Hazel also halted. "Yes, you're right. Whatever it is, I don't like it any more than you do. Still, we can't hang about here. Let's go on slowly and keep a good lookout."

The three rabbits approached the corner of the wood cautiously. They were a short distance away when Bigwig stopped again. "On the path, Hazel-rah. Something black, quite large. Can you see it?"

Hazel went a few yards nearer, peering ahead.

"Yes, I can see it. Surely it can't be what I think it is."

"Whatever it is," said Bigwig, "it's not moving. I don't think it's seen us, do you?"

"No," replied Hazel. "But I don't think it's alive at all."

"A trap?"

"No, it's not a trap. Still, whatever it is, we've got to go past it to get home."

They went forward yard by yard, Flyairth following Hazel somewhat hesitantly, till suddenly they both stopped at the same instant.

Beside the track, motionless in the clear moonlight, lay a man. He was on his side and fully clothed, including boots and a woolen cap. From the scuffled snow, they could see that he had been dragged the short distance from the footpath. His eyes were closed, and his face looked, in some way, distorted.

"Let him alone," said Bigwig. "I don't care whether he's dead or not. Let's just let him alone."

Flyairth, who was plainly nervous, remained with Bigwig, while Hazel went a little closer, sniffing. "He's not dead. I can just feel his breath. But I agree about letting him alone."

"Look at the snow," said Bigwig. "D'you see? There were two of them walking together side by side. Then this one fell down—suddenly, I'd say—and the other dragged him to where he is now and then left him and went on, the same way that they'd been going."

"Hadn't we better go back?" said Flyairth. "It must be dangerous, surely? Men—even one like this—they're always dangerous."

"No, no, it's all right," said Bigwig impatiently. "Anyway, we're here now."

They turned away and went down into the Honeycomb and through it to the sleeping burrows, where the first rabbit they came upon was Holly.

"Everything all right down at the bottom, Hazel-rah?"

"Yes, fine. This is Flyairth, by the way. She's joining us. What I need just at the moment is to talk to Vilthuril and Fiver. Can you get hold of them, Holly?"

As soon as Vilthuril and Fiver joined them, Hazel and Bigwig took them back into the Honeycomb, to avoid meeting anyone else before they were ready. Flyairth came with them.

"This is going to be a surprise for you, Vilthuril," said Hazel. "Who do you think this is? You'll never guess, so I'll tell you. Flyairth, from Thinial."

Fiver was as much surprised as Vilthuril.

"Why has she come here?" asked Holly. "Does she know about us?"

"No, but she'll tell you all about it herself later. I've told her she can stay, and a few other rabbits she brought with her. What we have to do just now is to get everybody in here ready to go down to the holes at the bottom. Will you tell them?"

The rabbits gathered in the Honeycomb, full of curiosity as Hazel's news spread.

"Who are the other rabbits with her?" Hyzenthlay asked him.

"I'm not sure yet, but just her own family, I think. Her last litter."

"Has she told you how she got here? Or how she's come to be here at all, for the matter of that?"

"It's too long a story to tell now. You can ask her tomorrow. Is everyone here? Let's get on down the hill."

He went across to the mouth of one of the runs, Flyairth and Bigwig following him. As soon as he had got his head outside, however, he stopped dead, listening tensely.

"What is it, Hazel-rah?" asked Bigwig. "What's the matter?"

"A hrududu," replied Hazel, "coming straight up here, very fast. See the lights?"

As he, Flyairth and Bigwig peered from the mouth of the hole, the hrududu approached, bouncing and skidding up the track toward them. Flyairth, trembling, turned and would have bolted back among the rabbits below if Bigwig had not restrained her.

"We're not in danger," said Bigwig sharply. "Pull yourself together. This is no time to go tharn, with everybody wondering what's going on. Keep still."

Flyairth, though she seemed half crazy with terror, did what she was told as the hrududu reached the trees and came to a stop a few yards away.

"It's because of that man lying in the snow," said Bigwig. "They've come for him. That's what it is."

Even before the hrududu had slithered to a halt and begun reversing, two men jumped out and ran over to where the man was lying.

"Get his shoulders, David. I'll take his legs."

"But is he alive?"

"Don't know. Let's get him into the jeep first."

Between them, the two men managed to lift their heavy burden into the jeep.

"Not too fast going back, Alan. I want to have a look at him. Anyway, we don't want to shake him about more than we can help."

The hrududu set off in the direction from which it had come, and quiet returned. It was a considerable time, however, before Hazel and Bigwig took the other rabbits out onto the Down and toward its foot. Flyairth was staggering and could hardly keep up: it was only with the encouragement of Hyzenthlay that she was able to reach the concealed holes at the bottom.

Hazel took several of his veterans into the one where he had left Bluebell and Pipkin. Hyzenthlay, with Flyairth, followed him. The burrow was now crammed full, but no one complained or tried to leave.

Hazel lay down in the dark beside Hyzenthlay. After some time, Vilthuril, close by, whispered to him, "Is Flyairth really here?"

"Yes, just on the other side of me. Do you want to tell her about your secret river in Efrafa?"

"No, not now. It would be better, wouldn't it, if I told her later?"

"Yes, I think you're right. She's better left alone for the moment. She's had enough surprises for one day."

If the other rabbits had been expecting Hazel to speak to them about the newcomers, they were disappointed. Neither he nor Bigwig said anything more by way of explaining Flyairth's arrival. Hazel simply went to sleep, and soon everyone else did the same. Flyairth remained restless and nervous for some time, but as the burrow grew warmer from the natural heat of so many bodies, she gradually relaxed and slept as soundly as the rest. In the middle of the night Hazel woke, slipped outside and went into both the other burrows to be sure that all was well. Finding that it was, he did not go back to his place beside Hyzenthlay but simply went to sleep again where he found himself.

Next day he made no special effort to question Flyairth but, having gone outside in a more or less hopeless attempt to silflay, went back to drowsing underground, like any other rabbit in winter. In the course of the day, several rabbits, both bucks and does, asked him whether he meant to tell them anything about the mysterious circumstances of Flyairth's arrival among them, but he simply replied that they were free to ask her and that the more rabbits she could talk to and get to know, the better for her and for them: as far as he was concerned, she was no different from any other rabbit. Only to Fiver did he say more.

"What do you make of her?"

"There's something unusual about her," replied Fiver. "She's no ordinary rabbit. She's got a lot on her mind: a lot that she's not going to talk about—or not yet, anyway. But whatever it is, she doesn't mean us any harm. And she's not crazy, like that poor Silverweed in Cowslip's warren. I think you're right to leave her alone to settle in and see what happens. Something unusual *will* happen; I'm sure of that, and so is Vilthuril. But obviously we can't send her away in all this snow and bitter cold. Let's see how she gets on with our rabbits. That'll tell us a good deal, for a start. We don't need to treat her in any special way; or not yet, anyhow."

That afternoon Flyairth approached Hazel on her own account.

"Hazel-rah, why weren't you and Bigwig afraid of the men last night? I was more frightened than I've ever been in my life."

"Oh, well, we're more or less used to them, you see," replied Hazel. "I was sure they wouldn't hurt us."

"But *men*, as close as that? It's not natural to rabbits. It *must* be dangerous."

Hazel said nothing more, and after a short time Flyairth asked, "Have all the rabbits come down now?"

"Yes," replied Hazel. "There's no one up there now. We shan't go back until it gets warmer."

"Of course, I didn't get a chance to see very much last night. Will you take me back there? Some of the rabbits have been describing the warren to me, and I'd like to see it again."

"Now?" asked Hazel rather soporifically.

She was downright. "Yes. Well, before it gets dark."

Hazel, good-natured as ever, agreed to go, and persuaded Bigwig to join them. The three set out, climbed the steep slope and went across to the footpath and the trees. The snow, frozen hard, was still lying, and Flyairth looked closely at the prints left by the men and the hrududu.

"Do men walk along this path very often?" she asked.

"In summer they do, quite a lot."

Flyairth followed them the few yards to the holes leading down into the Honeycomb. She was full of admiration and looked closely at the run in which Bigwig had fought and beaten General Woundwort.

"These Efrafan rabbits—they'd come to beat you, had they, and take the warren away from you?"

They told her about the dog, and how Hazel had been brought back from the farm.

"That's wonderful," she said. "What courage! Weren't you afraid?"

"We were all of us afraid," said Hazel. Not wishing to seem to be boasting, he went on, "It was really El-ahrairah who saved us. Dandelion'll tell you all about it, if you care to ask him. He's the rabbit for telling stories."

After they had looked at the sleeping burrows and were about to go back down the hill, she paused at the mouth of Kehaar's run and again gazed about her.

"You say men come along that path—as close to you as that? And they haven't done you any harm?"

"There's no particular reason why they should," answered Bigwig. "They don't grow flayrah or anything up here."

"But they must know you're here. The Blindness—aren't you afraid of the Blindness?"

"No. I don't think the men mind us being here."

"Men could destroy you all by giving you the Blindness. You know that?"

"They might, I suppose," replied Hazel, "but we don't think they will."

Flyairth said no more on the subject. As they went back down the hill, she returned to the question of how Bigwig had known her name and the name of Thinial. She evidently felt sure he could tell her more if he wanted to, but although he did not actually rebuff her, she got no more out of him.

Later on, when they were alone together, Hazel asked Bigwig how he had come to know in the first place that she was Flyairth, come from Thinial.

"Well, when Vilthuril was telling us the other night about Thinial and the doe who was Chief Rabbit, I formed a very vivid picture of her in my mind," replied Bigwig, "and then when we found Flyairth in our burrow, she looked and smelled exactly as I'd imagined."

"I can't help wishing you hadn't come out with it so sharply," said Hazel. "Now she thinks we're magic mind readers."

"Well, so we are," answered Bigwig, "thanks to Vilthuril. It won't do any harm to let Flyairth think so. I know she was afraid last night, but all the same, she's got a very strong mind of her own, that one. She'll be all over us if we're not careful."

The frost continued day after day, and there were more falls of snow. The rabbits were able to endure the cold but grew desperately hungry, until even Bluebell could not make a joke of it. Blackavar led a few of the does on an expedition to the farm, but they were able to pick up very little, chiefly on account of the cats. Most of the rabbits stayed underground, huddled together; even Holly and Bigwig were glad of a share in what little warmth was to be had.

One night, when Hyzenthlay, Vilthuril and Thethuthin-nang were pressing together against Hazel, Fiver and Big-wig, Vilthuril said, "Has Flyairth told you how she left Thinial and came to be here?"

"No, she hasn't," replied Bigwig. "I was going to ask her, straight out, to tell us, only Hazel thought she'd be better left alone until she felt more settled here."

"Well, she's told me," said Vilthuril, "and she didn't ask me not to tell anyone else. I think she'd probably be glad if I did tell you, so that *she* didn't have to. She seemed almost ashamed of herself, somehow; though I couldn't see that she had anything to be ashamed of, and so I told her."

"Have you said anything to her yet about your secret river?" asked Hazel.

"No. But I'd rather she did hear it from one of us—the three of us who actually knew about it in Efrafa. At the moment, she can't imagine how we came to know about her, so naturally she feels—well, uneasy, with us knowing something about her as big as that, and her still in the dark about it."

"Yes, it'll be better if you tell her yourself," said Hazel. "But about her leaving Thinial, how did that happen?"

"Well," said Vilthuril, "you remember I told you how we learned from the secret river that she was furiously angry when some of the rabbits in Thinial brought the young family of that poor rabbit—what was her name—"

"Milmown," prompted Hyzenthlay.

"Yes, of course, Milmown. They brought her young

family into Thinial and gave them a burrow. Flyairth tried to make them leave, but their friends were too many for her, and her position as Chief Rabbit was weakened by losing that argument. That was the last thing I ever learned from the river.

"Now she's told me herself that as the days went by she gradually lost more authority, not so much because of Milmown's family as because she couldn't think of anything but the White Blindness. She was obsessed by it and was continually putting forward ideas for preventing its getting into Thinial: ideas which most of her Owsla thought would be nothing but a nuisance; unnecessary things, they thought, which would only inconvenience everyone in the warren when there was no need. If only she'd dropped her obsession with the Blindness, they'd have forgotten about their quarrel with her.

"But she didn't. And one day when the Owsla had refused to accept an idea she'd proposed, she said something quite fatal. She said that if they wouldn't accept it she'd leave Thinial and take her family with her. Although they all felt she'd be a great loss, they still wouldn't accept what she was proposing, and so she had to go.

"It was late summer, quite warm, and she and her family were able to spend most nights in the open. And as for elil, she told me that she fought and killed a weasel herself. Somehow or other she'd heard of Efrafa, and she decided to go there. She didn't know what it was really like, of course. She'd only heard that it was a strictly run warren, and she thought that would suit her and that she'd be able to get herself accepted.

"Well, the next thing she heard was that Woundwort and the Efrafans had been beaten by us here. So she changed her plan and decided to come to us. But by the time she'd reached the foot of the Down, her young ones were worn out—they'd been wandering for hrair days, she told me—and when she happened to come upon these burrows down here, all clean and empty, she naturally decided to take one of them over. By the time you found her, she'd already been living here for quite a few days, and she'd come to consider the place her own. Still, she's happy enough with us, 'if only this terrible cold would let up,' as she said."

"We all like her very much," put in Thethuthinnang. "She really is the nicest rabbit anyone could hope to meet. She's made plenty of friends already. She's so good-natured and kind."

"If only she hadn't got this obsession with the Blindness," said Hyzenthlay. "I asked her the other day whether she didn't think that the time had come to forget about it, but she only asked me whether I'd ever seen a rabbit with the Blindness."

"And have you?" asked Bigwig.

"You know I haven't."

"I'm afraid of it too, come to that," said Hazel.

"Yes, but you don't think about it all the time. Flyairth does. It's her only fault, I'd say. What do you think, Fiver?"

"I think like her—if only this cold would let up,"

answered Fiver. "These are very harsh conditions we're living under. As soon as we can get back to our normal life, the sooner we'll be able to make up our minds about her."

"My mind's made up now," said Hyzenthlay. "I think she's one of the cleverest and most sensible rabbits I've ever known. Thinial—it's their loss and our gain, if you ask me."

A few days later Hazel and his veterans were much saddened by the death of Acorn, one of the original band who had come with him from Sandleford. The cold and hunger had finally proved too much for him. Even Bigwig, who had never particularly cared for Acorn, felt the loss keenly. "To think we brought him all that way, Hazel-rah, and he fought the Efrafans with us and came down the river on the boat, and now he stops running here. I shall miss him, I really shall."

"We all shall," answered Hazel. "I hope to goodness he's the only one we lose. They all look so thin and frozen that I wouldn't be surprised if more of them stopped running."

However, Hazel was able to set his fears aside when, a few days later, a thaw began. The snow and ice patches melted into water, which first trickled and then came pouring off the Down to form a small stream at the foot. Everyone was for returning to the Honeycomb immediately, but Hazel waited another day, until he was sure that the thaw was complete and that the frost would not return.

Once he had had the advice of Kehaar and felt certain of this, his first thought was for the resumption of the new warren project. With the gull's help in acting once more as go-between, he and Bigwig met Campion on the site. Campion having warmly approved of it, they agreed that rabbits from both warrens should meet there in two or three days' time. Groundsel (one of the former Efrafan officers who had been accepted into Hazel's warren after the defeat of Woundwort the previous summer) was to be Chief Rabbit, with Buckthorn, Strawberry and the Efrafan Captain Avens as the nucleus of his Owsla.

There were probably about ten or twelve rabbits who made the journey from Watership, with Bigwig to guide them. On his return, he told Hazel that they seemed to have mingled with the Efrafans quite happily. The elil had so far left them alone. No one had been killed, and digging in the bank was off to a good start. Hazel felt content to leave the business to Groundsel, at any rate for the time being, and turn his attention once more to his own warren.

Flyairth, he noticed, had apparently become the center of a group largely made up of the younger does who had escaped from Efrafa with Hyzenthlay. She looked cheerful in their company and seemed—or so he thought—to have won their respect. They appeared to be treating her deferentially and were clearly gratified by the warmth and friendliness with which she answered them. Falling into talk with one of the does, a youngster named Flesca, he asked her how she got on with Flyairth.

"Oh, we've all become good friends with her, Hazel-rah," said Flesca. "She's told us a lot about the warren she came from and how she and another doe started it. She was Chief Rabbit, apparently, and her Owsla were all does. I've never heard of anything like that, have you?"

"No, I haven't," replied Hazel, "but I'm not altogether surprised. I'm glad you all like her so much."

"Well, she's so amusing," said Flesca, "and she obviously likes being here with us. We've been telling her about the escape from Efrafa, and how Kehaar flew at General Woundwort to help us to get away. She said she wished she'd been there herself and had wings like Kehaar. A flying rabbit would really be something new, she said. And then she asked me whether I couldn't get her a pair of wings and another for myself, and we'd fly to Efrafa together. I couldn't help laughing."

The prolonged frost had left so little edible grass near the warren that one afternoon Hazel took out a search party—anyone who wanted to come—along the Down to try to find something better. Flyairth was eager to join and brought two or three does with her, as well as her young family.

Even along the crest of the Down the going was very wet, with small puddles everywhere. They found a good deal of coarse grass, which was edible if not particularly appetizing. While looking for fresh patches, they became quite widely scattered, but no one felt at risk. The Down lay empty all around, and the breeze brought no scent of elil but only the familiar smells of juniper and thyme. After the days of restriction in the frost-bound burrows, the spaciousness was exhilarating, and several of the rabbits began leaping and chasing one another almost like hares. Hazel felt the release as fully as anyone and joined happily in a mock fight with Speedwell and Silver in and out of the junipers. Running away from Speedwell, he ran down the steep north-facing slope, pulled up sharply in front of a thornbush and lost his balance, rolling over against a sodden tussock.

Picking himself up, Hazel, with a shock, saw a dog racing uphill toward him, yapping with excitement. It was a smooth-haired fox terrier, white with brown patches, soaking wet and muddy from the ditches and furrows down below. Hazel turned, breaking into his limping run, but even as he put on his best speed he knew that he was not fast enough; the dog was gaining on him. Desperately he changed direction, dodging one way and another, and as he did he felt the dog's breath panting closer, almost on top of him.

At this moment, another rabbit dashed down the slope and without pausing or checking its speed ran full tilt against the dog's left side. Both dog and rabbit fell, struggling together in a confused mass. As the rabbit broke free, the dog, taken completely by surprise, scrambled to its feet but then, off balance on the steep slope, fell again and rolled onto its back. The rabbit, more agile, regained its footing and ran off, while Hazel put a safe distance between himself and the dog.

The dog, getting up once more, looked about with a bewildered air but then, as a human voice called from below, made off downhill, none the worse physically but plainly in no mood for any further pursuit of rabbits.

Hazel felt scarcely less bewildered. The shock of the dog's sudden pursuit and its abrupt ending in his unexpected escape had left him confused. He limped a few steps uphill but then stopped, uncertain where to go and knowing only that he was safe. After some moments, he became aware that another rabbit was beside him and speaking to him. "Are you all right, sir? Would you like me to go along with you for a bit?" It was Flyairth.

"Was it—was it you that knocked the dog over?" he asked.

"Yes. Well, the slope was all in our favor, wasn't it?"

"I've never known a rabbit to attack a dog before."

"Well, it wasn't really an attack, was it? It was easy enough to knock it over, but I wasn't going to stay there to be bitten. Still, fortunately for us, its master called it away."

"You saved my life."

"Not too sure of that, but I'm glad to have helped you. Let's get back to the top, shall we? It must be about time we were going home."

Back in his own burrow in the Honeycomb, Hazel slept for a time but then went in search of Bigwig and Fiver. He found them both in Bigwig's burrow, together with Hyzenthlay and Vilthuril.

He told them what had happened.

"That must have taken some courage," said Bigwig. "I don't know whether I'd have done it, even for you, Hazel-rah. She's got plenty of weight, of course. But Frith in the rain! To go for a dog! Woundwort tried it, and look what happened to him."

"That was a much bigger dog," said Hazel. He turned to Vilthuril. "You had one or two things you wanted to ask her, hadn't you? About your secret river. I'll go and see if I can find her."

"Chief Rabbits don't go themselves: they send someone," said Bigwig.

Hazel made no reply but disappeared down the run outside the burrow.

When Flyairth had settled down among them, Hazel said, "I've told these rabbits what you did for me this afternoon. You saved my life, and I shan't forget it."

"I don't think any of us will forget it," said Bigwig. "Do you often do that sort of thing?"

"I've never had the chance before," replied Flyairth. "It was just on the spur of the moment, really. I'm not at all sure I'd dare to do it again. Let's leave it at that, shall we?"

"Well, we've asked you to come here for Vilthuril to tell you about something completely different," said Hazel. "How much have you heard about what's been called the secret river in Efrafa?"

"Practically nothing," replied Flyairth. "I've heard it mentioned once or twice, but not by anyone who claimed to know much about it."

"Well, Vilthuril will tell you now."

Vilthuril recounted again how she came upon the secret river and the extraordinary way in which she, Hyzenthlay and Thethuthinnang learned about Flyairth and Prake's starting the warren called Thinial, with its Owsla of does. She said as little as possible about Flyairth's preoccupation with the White Blindness, but spoke of Milmown and her litter and how after Milmown's death the young rabbits had been brought into Thinial against Flyairth's will.

"And as you'll remember telling me yourself," she concluded, "you and your young rabbits left Thinial because the Owsla couldn't agree with you about taking steps to guard against the White Blindness. You were going to Efrafa, but Frith be thanked you came here instead."

For a time Flyairth said nothing, as though unable to take in the extraordinary nature of what Vilthuril had told her about the secret river. At last she said, "Of course what you say must be true, or else you couldn't have known about Thinial and about poor Milmown and the quarrel with my Owsla. And yet—and yet how *can* it be true? I've never heard of anything like your secret river. It's struck me all of a heap, to tell you the truth."

"Thought transference," said Fiver. "Kehaar knows about it. He told me it's common among birds who live in flocks, like seagulls."

"But to go all that distance—"

"Kehaar told me that men have even more incredible

ways of telling news to one another. Hrair miles through the air, he said."

Seeing her still perplexed and also, he thought, a little petulant at not being able, like the other rabbits, to accept the idea of the secret river, Hazel said, "Well, let's not bother about it now. I'm sure I'm as much in the dark as anyone else. There were two questions we wanted to ask you, Flyairth, but I think we already know the answer to one of them. Was anyone in Thinial sending out knowledge, which our rabbits got from the river? The answer to that is, as far as you know, no one. And the second question is: How far away is Thinial? Where is it?"

"It must be a long, long way from here," answered Flyairth, "toward the sunset. My family and I, we took hrair days getting here."

"Neither you nor anyone else could go back there?"

"Oh, no. Much too far."

"Kehaar could probably find it," put in Bigwig.

"But we don't need to know," said Hazel. "All I wanted to know was whether other rabbits from Thinial might turn up here. The answer is that that's extremely unlikely."

"Hazel-rah," said Flyairth, "why was it that you didn't ask me whether I'd like to join Groundsel and the rabbits he took to the new warren? I'd gladly have gone with them, only I never heard anything about it. Once the thaw began they were gone so quickly."

"Well, I'm afraid it never occurred to me to ask you," answered Hazel. "You see, we already knew which of our rabbits were going, before the frost began. The whole thing was settled and our rabbits would have left here before you'd joined us, if it hadn't been for the frost. When the thaw began, we just took the whole business up where we'd left off."

"So few rabbits went with Groundsel," she said. "If it had been up to me, I'd have taken the whole warren."

"Only you didn't happen to be Chief Rabbit, did you?" said Bigwig.

"I'd gladly have gone with him myself." And then, after a pause, "Hazel-rah, there's something I want to say to your Owsla; something very important. Only, in this warren I can't make out who's in the Owsla and who isn't. I'm confused."

"Well, that's our fault," replied Hazel. "You see, we came here together and went through all sorts of danger together, like beating General Woundwort; and we've never needed an Owsla for giving out orders and that sort of thing. We're all in the Owsla, really. It works, anyway."

"Yes, I know it works," said Flyairth. "You're all so contented and get on with each other so well. No one has any enemies, as far as I can tell."

"Well," said Hazel, "what is your important thing? You can tell us and we'll listen seriously, I promise you."

"I think you already know what it is," replied Flyairth. "The White Blindness. None of you seem to know what it's like, or to realize your dreadful danger. None of you has ever seen a rabbit with the Blindness, or seen the Blindness spread in a warren. It's unbelievably horrible—by far the most horrible of all the things that threaten rabbits. Worse than all the Thousand put together. Rabbits still alive, turned into groping, rotting lumps of misery. I know you think I'm obsessed. So would you be if you'd seen what I've seen. How even men can be so cruel as to give rabbits the Blindness I can't imagine. Everything we plan, everything we do, ought to take into account the Blindness and how to avoid it."

She had spoken so forcefully and passionately that her audience was stunned into silence. At length Hazel said, "Well, what's your advice, then? What do you think we ought to do?"

"You're all in such terrible danger here," said Flyairth. "A warren right beside a path that humans use. I've never seen a warren so much exposed to danger."

"What's the matter, Fiver?" asked Hazel.

"*You* ought to know," answered Fiver. "You were there. I said almost exactly the same thing, long ago, to the Chief Rabbit of the Sandleford warren, and he wouldn't believe me. And what happened you know."

"So you think Flyairth's right?"

"Yes, of course she is. The only difference between then and now is that then I *knew* something terrible was going to happen—happen soon. But now, in spite of what she's said, I don't feel like that. I don't feel any dread of the future. But she's right, all the same."

"And what do you think we ought to do, Flyairth?"

"Leave here, all of us, and move to a safer place. A new warren in a safer place. And no men. What happened the other night in the snow, when the men came—that *can't* be right. I wouldn't have believed it if I hadn't seen it: I mean, that rabbits could even think they could live in such a place."

"Why, you've only been here a few days," broke in Bigwig angrily. "And here you are trying to tell us all what to do. Who do you think you are?"

"I'm sorry," answered Flyairth. "You asked me to tell you what was worrying me, and you've just asked me what I thought you ought to do. I was only answering your questions."

"Don't go for her, Bigwig," said Hazel. "I'm glad to know what she thinks. Flyairth, I'm afraid we can't send you or anyone else to Groundsel's warren just at present. It's all been agreed with Campion, you see. We'll drop it for now. I can feel it's warmer tonight, but let's go to sleep all together, where we are."

He did not himself, however, fall asleep immediately but lay awake between Bigwig and Fiver, turning over in his mind what Flyairth had said.

15

Flyairth's Departure

Abiit, excessit, evasit, erupit.
(She departed, she withdrew, she strode off, she broke forth.)

CICERO, *In Catilinam*

"Hazel-rah, she's doing everything she can to take over the leadership," said Bigwig. "She's at it now in the Honeycomb, telling all the young rabbits about the men in the snow the other night. She's telling them that as long as they stay here they're in deadly danger of the White Blindness, but that she'll lead them to a safe place and start a new warren. Shall I go back and kill her, now, before she does any more harm?"

"No, don't do that," answered Hazel. "Or not yet, anyway."

"What it comes to," said Bigwig, "is that she used to be a Chief Rabbit—huh, a *doe* as Chief Rabbit!—until they threw her out, and now she's come here she means to be Chief Rabbit again."

"Were any of our Sandleford rabbits listening to her?" asked Hazel.

"No, nor was Blackavar either. But a lot of the youngsters were, and some of the Efrafan does as well."

"I'd like to talk to Fiver and Blackberry," said Hazel. "Vilthuril and Hyzenthlay too, come to that. Let's go and find them, come on."

They found them, as well as Thethuthinnang, crowded together in Fiver's burrow, dozing in the warmth of their bodies.

"Bigwig," said Hazel, "tell them what you just told me about Flyairth."

Bigwig did so, working himself, if anything, into a still greater rage. "She's got to be killed," he ended. "She's got to be killed *soon*, before she does any more harm."

"Well, hang on a moment or two," said Blackberry. "Hazel-rah, can I say a few things?"

"Yes, and Fiver as well," said Hazel.

"This fuss, as far as I can make out," said Blackberry, "is all about the Blindness. Bigwig thinks that what Flyairth wants first and foremost is to become a Chief Rabbit again. I don't think it is. I think that if she'd never come across the Blindness but had left her own warren all the same and come here, she'd have settled in quite peacefully, without making any trouble."

"She was Chief Rabbit in that Thinial warren of hers before ever she came across the Blindness," said Bigwig. "Now she wants to be Chief Rabbit again. All her talk about the Blindness is just a pretext to get support."

"Well, anyway, she wants to persuade as many rabbits

as she can to move out of here," said Blackberry. "And the reason, she says, is that here there's great danger from the Blindness. Now listen. As far as I've ever been able to make out, men only infect rabbits with the Blindness when the rabbits have become a nuisance to them: eating their green-stuff, tearing the bark off their fruit trees, spoiling their lettuces and all that. If we'd gone in for anything like that, they'd have infected us long ago. But they haven't, because so far we've been no real trouble to them, up here in this lonely place. There's nothing to spoil.

"But there's one other thing that would turn them against us. If there grew to be too many of us, that'd lead to trouble: if this whole place got to be full of rabbits, here, there and everywhere. If all the youngsters and all the Efrafan does were to stay here, there'd very soon be a whole crowd of rabbits, all over the Down and increasing all the time. The men wouldn't like that.

"Flyairth wants everyone to move to a new warren in a more lonely place. But there's no place so lonely that men won't get to know about it if there are too many rabbits there."

"Let her go," said Fiver. "Let her go and take as many youngsters with her as ever she can. The more she takes, the safer we'll be here. In fact, if she weren't obliging us by doing it herself, we might even have had to make her."

"But can anyone stay here who wants to?" asked Hyzenthlay.

"Yes, of course," said Hazel. "Until we get overcrowded

again, if we ever do. But we don't have to think about that for a long time. Fiver and Blackberry are right. Let Flyairth go."

Later that day, Flyairth left the Down by herself, saying that she was off to find a suitably safe place for a new warren. She had not asked anyone to come with her.

She was gone for three days. When she returned, she told Hazel that she had found a much safer and more secluded place. She asked him to come with her to look at it. Hazel replied, quite amiably, that going to a new warren formed no part of his plans for the moment, but she was free to invite anyone else she wished.

However, she did not make a second reconnaissance, but the next day set off with a considerable number of the younger rabbits, whom she had convinced that they were in danger where they were. She was not, she said, coming back.

The weather continued to improve, and there were more warm days. One fine evening Hazel and a number of his friends, including Hyzenthlay, Vilthuril and Thethuthinnang, were lying peacefully in the sun.

"I wonder how Flyairth and her lot are getting on," said Holly. "And for the matter of that, where they are."

"Kehaar'll be back any day now," said Bigwig. "He'll find out where they've gone and how Flyairth's getting on as Chief Rabbit."

"Well enough, I should imagine," said Dandelion. "You know, I couldn't help liking her. She was most amusing to talk to and had a lot of good ideas."

"She saved my life," said Hazel, "but she never boasted about it to anyone."

"I'd imagine she'd be a very good Chief Rabbit," said Silver, "as long as she had a male partner to—well, you know—to balance her when she needed it."

"I like the idea of a female Chief Rabbit," said Hazel. "Seriously, I think we ought to have one. Hyzenthlay, how would you like to take it on?"

"I wish you would," said Blackavar. "I think all of us would be only too pleased."

Hyzenthlay was about to decline with a joke, when, glancing round, she realized that they were all looking at her expectantly, full of support for what Hazel had proposed.

"Tell us you will," said Fiver.

"Well, if Hazel will stay on with me, I will," she answered. "And I promise —"

"Yes? Yes?" said three or four of them together.

"I promise to be the biggest nuisance he's ever met in his life, and to disagree with him about everything!"

"I feel more lighthearted already," said Hazel, touching his nose to hers.

When the news spread through the warren, there was not a dissentient voice. Everyone, even Bigwig, had confidence in Hyzenthlay, particularly those Efrafan does who had not left with Flyairth.

*

Spring was fine and dry, and summer came in, full of promise and ease. One beautiful afternoon, as Bluebell, Hawkbit and three or four others were at silflay on the Down, a stranger rabbit, looking distinctly tired, came lolloping up to them over the grass.

"I've been sent with a message from Efrafa," he said. "Can you take me to your Chief Rabbit?"

"Certainly," replied Bluebell. "Male or female? We cater for all tastes here, you know."

16

Hyzenthlay in Action

By any reasonable plan
I'll make you happy, if I can;
My own convenience count as *nil*;
It is my duty, and I will.

w. s. gilbert, "Captain Reece"

As it happened, however, the Efrafan messenger, despite Bluebell's fulsome welcome, found that he had no choice in the matter of a Chief Rabbit. Hazel was not in the warren that afternoon, having taken Silver and Blackberry with him for a cautious look round Nuthanger Farm. Since the defeat of Woundwort, Hazel had always retained, at the back of his mind, an irrational—indeed, a superstitious—idea that in some way or other the farm was of lucky import for himself and his rabbits. Of course, this did not mean that he disregarded the ever-present danger from the cats and the dog, but he felt intuitively that the whole place, treated with proper and knowledgeable respect, welcomed him, much as an experienced sailor might feel that the sea, regarded as it ought to be, was beneficial rather than hostile:

a potential for good. He liked to see what was going on at the farm, even though most of it was beyond his understanding. In summer he used to pay it periodic visits, taking with him one or two reliable rabbits and always returning with the notion that the time had been well spent and had tipped some sort of recondite balance in his favor.

That was what he was up to this afternoon. He had left Hyzenthlay in charge—not that anything was likely to happen—and gone down the hill in carefree spirits. Consequently, it was Hyzenthlay to whom Bluebell conducted the visitor.

His message was not really one of any particular moment. Efrafa was once again getting rather overcrowded with does, and Campion had picked out a number who had actually told him, of their own accord, that they would welcome a chance to broaden their horizon and see what life was like on Watership Down. As far as Campion was concerned, they could stay there or come back, as they pleased. Feeling sure that Hazel would have no objection to the idea, he had told them to set off from Efrafa whenever they liked. It then occurred to him that none of them knew the way. There was, however, in Efrafa a young buck named Rithla, who had come to Campion a few months before with a message from Hazel and had remained there, having found a doe with whom he had mated happily and fathered a litter. Campion had now seen in him a guide for the emigrating does. He had also, on second thoughts, felt that it would be only polite to let Hazel know in advance that the does were coming. He had therefore told Rithla to guide them as far as the Belt, from where it would be easy for them to continue on their own to Watership, and then, leaving them to rest and feed, himself to press on and tell Hazel that they were on their way.

All this Rithla explained to Hyzenthlay, sitting with her in the Honeycomb, together with Thethuthinnang, Bigwig and a few more who happened to be about.

Hyzenthlay, not having been a Chief Rabbit for very long, was anxious to act conscientiously and to make a really good job of anything that came her way. Accordingly she told Rithla, on her own authority, that the does would be most welcome (more especially since a considerable number of does had gone off with Flyairth). Upon learning that he had left them all on the Belt, to come on in their own time, she said that she thought this was rather dangerous. In spite of Campion's instructions to Rithla, she thought, first, that they might mistake their way and get lost and, second, that in the open they were in danger from elil. She would therefore go out herself to meet them and bring them in before nightfall. No, she would not need Rithla to guide her. The way was plain enough. He was tired and ought to silflay and then sleep.

Bigwig, who had overheard most of what she said, at once began to protest. How could she be sure of meeting the does? More important, there was any amount of danger from elil for a rabbit alone on the Down. Rithla had been lucky. He should never have been told to come on by himself. Hyzenthlay ought to remain where she was.

Hyzenthlay replied that if the does were already on their way, there would be no difficulty in finding them. There was only one way, and it was plain enough, a humans' footpath. As for elil, she could run faster than they could, and anyway she did not expect to meet any by day.

Bigwig then said that he and Holly would go with her, but this she declined. She did not want any other rabbits to risk themselves.

At this, Bigwig lost his temper. "You call yourself a Chief Rabbit and then say you're going out traipsing about by yourself for the sake of a few miserable Efrafan does. Is that what you call weighing one thing with another? If Hazel were here, he'd certainly forbid you, and well you know it. A stupid, fatheaded doe calling herself Chief Rabbit! Chief Field Mouse more like."

Hyzenthlay went up to him and looked him squarely in the eye. "Bigwig, I've said what I'm going to do, and that's all there is to it. If you reject my authority over this, there'll be no authority left in the warren by tomorrow, as you must know perfectly well. Now please let me get on; and have some clean burrows ready for the Efrafan does when they arrive."

Bigwig, fuming, stormed out of the Honeycomb and began cursing the first rabbit he met, who happened to be Hawkbit. Meanwhile, Hyzenthlay, leaving Thethuthinnang to tell Hazel, as soon as he returned, what had happened, set off toward the Belt.

She was surprised not to meet the Efrafan rabbits on the way and wondered what could possibly have happened to them. It was now early evening. What breeze there had been had dropped. The air was still. The shadows of the tall cow parsley were growing longer, and the sun was dropping toward a cloud bank in the west. With a certain misgiving she pressed on. After quite some time, she found herself approaching the Belt, with no sign of rabbits anywhere. She began searching to right and left, but found no trace in the twilight. As she was wondering what to do, she came upon a female hare feeding its leverets in the form. The hare spoke first.

"Are you looking for some stray rabbits? Does? There's a small crowd over there, by that beech tree."

A few moments later Hyzenthlay was among them.

"I'm a Watership rabbit come to look for you. Rithla told us you were going to make your own way to us. What's happened?"

"It's Nyreem here," answered one of the does. "She's hurt one of her back legs and can't use it at all. We've stayed with her. We weren't going to leave her out alone all night for the elil."

Hyzenthlay examined the injured rabbit. She was in a lot of pain and could barely stand, let alone walk. The upper part of the leg was swollen and very tender. However, there was no wound, and Hyzenthlay thought that all she needed was rest. She said so.

"Rest? Here?" said another doe. "How long for?"

"Until she's better," answered Hyzenthlay shortly.

"But it's nightfall now. If an enemy comes, she can't run, can't defend herself—"

"*I* am going to stay with her," said Hyzenthlay. "The rest of you are all to get on as fast as you can, up that track—that one over there. That will take you straight to Watership, where they're expecting you. No arguments now! Get on with it!"

The does, none of whom had ever been a hundred yards beyond Efrafa in their lives, obeyed her with no more than a show of reluctance, and Hyzenthlay settled down beside Nyreem in the long grass. Pathetically young and totally inexperienced, the poor little creature was almost beside herself with fear, and it was all that Hyzenthlay could do to calm her and give her the reassurance that she by no means felt in herself. She told her all the stories she could remember and finally settled her to sleep, pressed up against her own warm flank. Soon she felt drowsy herself, but struggled against every inclination to drop off. Owls began calling, the moon rose, and from the grass came all the tiny noises of night—rustlings, susurrations, minute tappings and quick little here-and-gone sounds that might never have been at all, might have existed only in a pair of long ears strained to the limit with listening. She prayed with all her might to El-ahrairah for his protection and shelter, and tried to feel his presence with her among the moon shadows.

Now began one of the most frightening nights of her life. Cramped, and trying not to move for fear of disturbing Nyreem, despite herself she began to think of all that she had ever heard of the elil, of the silence with which they moved upwind, stalking their rabbit prey so noiselessly that the victim knew nothing until the pounce and the grip of teeth in the flesh. She had seen worms and beetles writhing in the beaks of the blackbirds, had seen thrushes cracking the shells of live snails on stones. Would it be like this for her? She had seen, too, the scavenger beetles that dug cavities and laid their eggs inside, together with bodies of small dead creatures for the hatched young to live on. Bats and owls, too, she thought of, hunting moths and mice, their living prey. Moles, she knew, would fight each other to the death when they met in their underground passages. Were rabbits the only creatures that did not hunt and kill? So it seemed in her dismal thoughts. Woundwort had done all he could to confer ferocity on rabbits, and little good it had done him in the end. She thought of all the Efrafans whom he had sent to their deaths. She wished with all her heart that Woundwort were lying beside her now. And if that was not desperation, what was?

The young doe beside her slept on soundly. If only, she thought, she could get her alive and well to the warren, she would have justified her own insistence on coming here alone. But in order to do that, she must herself survive, and there was nothing more she could do to bring that about.

She saw with surprise that the moon had almost set. She must have slept without knowing it; and nothing bad had happened. This was encouraging, and spontaneously she began to feel herself in a more cheerful frame of mind. El-ahrairah, she thought, would not leave a loyal rabbit helpless.

After a while, she had the notion that they were being watched. Even as she realized this, the long grass parted and there, before her eyes, was a rat.

For long moments in the fading moonlight they sized each other up. It was not a very large rat, though quite big enough. Also, it was plainly foraging. She could see on its bared teeth fragments of some sort of flesh. It blinked once or twice, twitched its whiskers and moved nearer. It was still undecided.

Hyzenthlay spoke in hedgerow vernacular. "This young doe mine. I mother. You come to kill, I fight till you dead." Instinctively she stood up, to bring home to the rat her superior size and height. At this, Nyreem woke and began to whimper.

Hyzenthlay placed herself between Nyreem and the rat. As she did so, a feathered mass, clawed and smelling of blood, fell upon them from above, without a sound. Instantly, before she even had time to be afraid, it was gone and the rat with it, horribly pierced in its talons.

"What's happened? Oh, what was it?" cried Nyreem, pressing close against her.

"An owl," replied Hyzenthlay. "It's gone away now. There's nothing to be afraid of, dear. I'm here. You go back to sleep."

She herself fell asleep again, this time thinking with a kind of sullen indifference that everything had happened which could happen and anyway she was past caring.

When she woke it was a little after sunrise, and a

blackbird was singing in the beech tree as though there were no such thing as fear in the world. Nyreem, too, woke, and she asked her whether the leg felt any better. The swelling had certainly gone down a good deal, and she was able to limp a few steps. Hyzenthlay told her to lie down again and go on resting. She herself went and had a look round, then bit off a burnet and some sorrel leaves, which they ate together, lying in the sunshine as it grew gradually warmer.

Hyzenthlay asked Nyreem why she had joined the rabbits leaving Efrafa. The little doe replied that she had wanted to be like Quiens, an older rabbit whom she greatly admired. "That's how I hurt my leg," she said. "Quiens jumped right down a steep bank and I followed her, but it was too much for me. I thought at first I'd broken my leg. I know it was a silly thing to do, but they were very kind about it. I do hope they all got safely to your warren last night."

As the sun climbed slowly toward ni-Frith, Hyzenthlay wondered whether to press Nyreem to do her best to go on. She certainly did not want them to spend another night in the open. It was a difficult decision, but it was one that would have to be made. Finally she thought that the thing to do would be to wait until the evening and then encourage Nyreem to do the best she could. Head in the grass, she settled down patiently to watch the insect world amid the sun and dew. She could perceive no purpose whatever in their clamberings among the grass blades. She herself lay so still that the blackbird, looking for something to eat, alighted beside her and pecked here and there for a while before fluttering on.

It was a very long day. The only movement was that of the thin grass shadows and of the clouds passing above. Both were so smooth and regular that they did nothing to break the monotony. During the late afternoon the heat slowly lessened, and she dozed once more, becoming alert only when a pair of goldfinches alighted close by, stripped the seeds from the taller grasses and bobbed restlessly away.

A few moments later she started up in alarm, raising her ears to listen tensely and looking one way and another with staring eyes. Some animal was coming through the grass, an animal fully as big as herself, if not bigger. It was downwind of her, and she could smell nothing; but she could see the disturbed grass moving in a steady progression toward her. Instinctively she crouched down, her back legs drawn up under her, ready to leap.

The next thing she knew, the long grass parted and Bigwig appeared.

"Bigwig!" cried Hyzenthlay, overcome with relief and feeling sure on the instant that all her problems were as good as solved. "Bigwig! Why ever are you here?"

"Oh, well, I—er—I was just—er—having a bit of a stroll, you know," replied Bigwig in some embarrassment. "I—er—thought you might be somewhere about, sort of. How are *you*?" he said, turning to Nyreem. "Leg better now? Your Efrafan friends are all waiting for you and hoping you'll be back with them this evening. Just see what you can do with it, because I think it's time we were going."

"Oh, I'm sure I'll be quite all right now, sir," answered Nyreem. "If we don't go too fast, I'm sure I'll manage very well, no danger."

"Good!" said Bigwig. "Come on, then. I'll keep on one side of you and—er"—he choked slightly—"Hyzenthlay-rah will keep on the other. You'll do fine."

They set off slowly, Nyreem hobbling as best she could, determined not to complain. As near as she could guess, this must be none other than Thlayli, the renowned captain of the Watership Owsla, who had defeated the terrible General Woundwort in underground combat. She stole a sideways glance. Yes, it must be he. He was scarred all over, and on his head was the tuft of fur which had given him his name. Had he actually come out to look for her? Or, more likely, for Hyzenthlay, who was talking across her and telling Thlayli about the rat and the owl. Apparently they regarded looking after her as all in a day's work and simply part of their duty as officers. They regarded themselves as responsible for any Watership rabbit, however insignificant. So this was what it meant to be a Watership rabbit? Then and there, she resolved never to do anything that might forfeit her place in the warren.

They arrived home a little before nightfall, to find Hazel and Silver pretending to be concluding a late silflay but in actuality watching out for them. Nyreem, almost too overawed to thank them, rejoined her Efrafan companions and told them about her adventure. Even Quiens seemed favorably impressed, and Nyreem could not help feeling that she had made quite a good start in the new warren.

17

Sandwort

For they are impudent children and stiffhearted.

EZEKIEL 2:4

After two or three days, Nyreem's injured leg had completely recovered and she had settled into the warren as smoothly as any of the new arrivals from Efrafa; that is, until the time when she became an admirer of Sandwort's.

Sandwort, a strongly built and self-willed young buck, was no more than a few months old when he began to attract criticism from several of the older rabbits.

"You'd better keep an eye on that young Sandwort of yours," remarked Silver one day to his mother, a quiet, gentle doe named Melsa, a descendant of Clover, one of the rabbits from Nuthanger Farm. "He was plain insolent to me this morning; I had to cuff him over the head."

"I can't do anything with him," replied Melsa. "He's got no respect for me, or for any other rabbit, come to that. The trouble is he's very big and strong for his age, and he's influenced quite a few of the younger rabbits to admire him and see him as a sort of leader."

"Well, you'd better tell him to think a bit less of himself," said Silver, "if he doesn't want to get on the wrong side of Hazel-rah and Bigwig; or of me either, for that matter." He liked Melsa and on that account was content to leave it there, for the moment, anyway.

It was Sandwort, however, who soon showed himself of no mind to leave it there. Before long, others among the veteran rabbits were complaining of his behavior. He had disregarded Holly, who had told him to get back out of sight in the long grass when men were coming up the Down. He had refused point-blank to obey Speedwell, a quiet and easygoing rabbit if ever there was one, when told one evening to take his scuffling companions out of the Honeycomb and find somewhere else to tussle and brawl. "We've got as much right to be here as you," he said; and Speedwell, faced by a small crowd of Sandwort's hangers-on, had felt it best to say no more and himself to leave the Honeycomb.

In short, it soon became plain that Sandwort did not regard himself as subordinate to any rabbit in the warren. In such a free-and-easy society this was not particularly obtrusive until he began persuading other young rabbits, both male and female, to accompany him on expeditions beyond the warren and refusing to say where they were going or where they had been.

"I don't have to tell you or any other rabbit where I've been," he replied one evening to Silver, who had met and questioned him returning with two or three others from what had evidently been a long and exhausting excursion. "I can go where I please and it's no one else's business."

On this occasion, however, he put himself in a false position, since not only Silver but several of the older rabbits noticed that he had come back with one rabbit fewer than he had taken out.

"Where's Crowla?" asked Silver, who earlier in the day had done his best to dissuade that young doe from accompanying Sandwort.

"How should I know?" replied Sandwort. "I don't have to answer for every rabbit who takes a notion to go out of the warren at the same time that I do."

"But wasn't she with you?" persisted Silver.

"She may have been, for all I know."

"Are you saying that you think it's nothing to do with you what may have happened to Crowla, who went out with you?"

"As far as I'm concerned, any rabbit's free to come and go as she pleases," said Sandwort. "I dare say she may come back a bit later."

However, Crowla did not come back, and after several days her friends were forced to conclude that she was not going to come back at all. Sandwort showed no particular concern and continued to say that whatever might have happened to her was nothing to do with him. It was at this point that Hazel felt obliged to take notice himself. That evening he tackled Sandwort at silflay on the Down.

"Did you invite Crowla to join you on this expedition you made?" he asked.

"No—*sir*," answered Sandwort, continuing to nibble the grass. "She asked me to let her come."

"And you agreed that she could?"

"I said she could please herself."

"But all the same, you saw her among the others when you set out. You knew she was there. When did you first notice that she wasn't there?"

"I can't remember. On the way back, I suppose."

"And you say you didn't feel that was any business of yours?"

"No, I didn't. I don't pick and choose which rabbits want to join me. That's their business, not mine."

"Even in a case like this? An inexperienced doe a good deal younger than yourself?"

"A lot of does are younger than myself."

"Answer me properly," said Hazel angrily. "Did you or didn't you think she was any business of yours? Yes or no?"

Sandwort paused. Finally he replied, "No, I didn't."

"That's all I wanted to know," said Hazel. "Nyreem was with you, too, that day, wasn't she?"

"Oh, I rather think she was."

"A completely inexperienced young doe just arrived from Efrafa with an injured leg?"

Sandwort made no reply.

"You didn't feel concerned on her account either?"

"No, not particularly."

Hazel left him without another word.

Later that evening, he talked the matter over with Fiver and Bigwig. "There's a nice young doe we've lost; one he led to her death. I liked Crowla. She was coming on very well. And he's quite likely to do it again, as far as I can see."

"Why don't I drag him out and beat the daylights out of him?" asked Bigwig.

"No," said Fiver. "That wouldn't really get us anywhere. That would only make him more of a rebel among his own friends. You see, strictly speaking, he hasn't done anything wrong. It's true enough that he can go out of the warren, go anywhere he likes; so can any rabbit, and if other rabbits choose to go at the same time, it's not his business to stop them. It's simply that no right-minded rabbit would act in such a way—particularly when one of his friends has gone missing as a result of going with him."

"Well, he's got to be stopped from doing it again," said Bigwig.

"The only way we could manage that," said Fiver, "would be to forbid him to leave the warren at all, except to silflay."

"I'm not prepared to go that far," said Hazel. "It's a bit too much like Woundwort. We'll have to let him alone for the time being. But if anyone else fails to come back from going out with him, we shall have to do something."

Sandwort's next objectionable act took place only a day or two later. It was not serious, like the loss of Crowla, but nevertheless it amounted to deliberate insolence. Silver and

Blackavar had been to the foot of the Down on some activity of their own and as they set out to return found that they were being followed by Sandwort and three or four other young rabbits. Silver and Blackavar had come to a half-closed gap between some thick tussocks of grass and were pausing, hesitant whether to push through it or to go round, avoiding the tussocks altogether. At this moment, Sandwort came up to them from behind and said, "Are you going through here?" Neither Silver nor Blackavar gave him any immediate reply. "Well, I am, anyway," said Sandwort, pushed them aside and went past them into the gap, followed by the other rabbits, one or two of whom did not bother to conceal their amusement.

Small incidents of this kind continued to occur, until it was plain that Sandwort was bringing them about deliberately whenever opportunity offered, usually in the presence of younger rabbits, who would gossip about them in the warren. On the only occasion when one of these led to blows, the older rabbit came off worse, Sandwort being strong and heavy. Another day, Holly overheard one of the youngsters talking about "Sandwort's Owsla." This, passed on to Bigwig, made him so angry that he had to be restrained from going to look for Sandwort then and there. "It wasn't him that said it," pointed out Hazel. "He'd only have a justified grievance against you and make all he could out of it afterward."

Before the whole matter of Sandwort's behavior could come to a head, however, it was eclipsed by an entirely different kind of crisis. One morning, an hour or two after sunrise, two young rabbits, Crowfoot and Foxglove, both friends of Sandwort's, came dashing into the warren in a state of panic, asking to speak to Hazel immediately.

"We were in the garden of the big house down the hill," said Crowfoot, "just the two of us and Sandwort. We were looking for flayrah, when all of a sudden this huge dog came dashing toward us, barking and growling. Sandwort immediately told us to separate, and we ran off in different directions as fast as we could. The dog didn't pursue us, so after a bit we came back to find Sandwort. And what's happened is that he's fallen into a kind of pit and can't get out."

"A pit?" said Hazel. "What sort of a pit?"

"It's a man-made pit," said Foxglove, "not quite so deep as a man's tall, and the sides are about the same length. The sides and the bottom are all perfectly smooth—smooth as a wall—not a foothold anywhere, and Sandwort's lying at the bottom."

"Injured?"

"We don't think so. We think he must have been running from the dog as fast as he could, like we were, and not looking where he was going, when he fell into the pit. There's hardly any water in it, and he's just lying there. He can't get out."

"And the sides are smooth and straight up and down, you say?" asked Hazel. "Well, if he can't get out by himself, I shouldn't think we can get him out, but I'll go and see. Blackberry, you come with me, will you, and Fiver? No one else is to come. I don't want a whole crowd attracting the dog back."

The three rabbits made their way to the foot of the Down, ran across the empty cornfield and the road, and went cautiously through the hedge into the big garden. It took them some time to find the pit of which Crowfoot had spoken. When at length they did, they could see nothing in the least likely to reassure them. The trench, about five feet by three and perhaps four feet in depth, was lined with smooth concrete. It had been dug out to serve the same purpose as a water butt. There were no steps down, but beside it lay a bucket attached to a rope. There were perhaps two or three inches of water in the bottom, and here Sandwort was lying on his side and holding up his head to breathe. He did not see them.

On the edge of the trench they were completely in the open, and as soon as they had taken in the discouraging situation, they went back under the cover of some nearby laurel bushes, where they conferred.

"We'll never get him out of there," said Blackberry. "It can't be done."

"Not with one of your brilliant schemes?" asked Hazel.

"I'm afraid not. There's no scheme can get him out of there. If a man were to come for water, I suppose he'd take him out and probably kill him, but that's not likely, is it? There's very little water in there."

"So he'll stay there and die?"

"I'm afraid he will. And it'll take some time too."

The three rabbits returned to the warren in low spirits. Hazel always hated the loss of any rabbit, but to know that Sandwort was beyond help and could only be left to die slowly was depressing in the extreme. The news had quickly run round the warren, and so many rabbits wanted to go and see Sandwort's plight for themselves that Hazel felt obliged to forbid any of them to go even as far as the Iron Tree at the foot of the Down.

"So he'll just have to be left to die?" asked Tindra, one of the does who had been close to him. "It'll take a long time, won't it?"

"I'm afraid it may," replied Hazel. "Three days, four days. I've never known anything like this before, and I simply can't tell."

All that day and the next, the idea of Sandwort lying in the pit was never far from the rabbits' thoughts. Even those, like Silver and Bigwig, who had had good reason to dislike him would have helped him escape from his dreadful predicament if only they could.

On the afternoon of the third day after the news had been brought to the warren, Tindra and Nyreem deliberately disobeyed Hazel, going furtively along the crest of the Down and then, after they had gone a considerable distance, to the foot. Young and inexperienced as they were, they became lost and wandered one way and another for some time before stumbling more or less by chance through the hedge and into the garden of the big house.

It did not take them very long to come upon the pit.

Sandwort, his eyes closed, was lying unmoving in the water. The flies were walking on his eyelids and ears, but every few seconds a minute release of bubbles showed that he was still breathing. Some sodden hraka lay by his tail.

The two does stared down at him. Although there was clearly nothing to be done, they remained in the open, fascinated and unmoving, for some time, until they were startled by the voices of approaching children. As they ran back into the laurels the children appeared, three or four of them together, pushing through the azaleas on the opposite side of the little glade. One of them, a boy of about eleven, broke into a run and jumped across the pit. On the further side he stopped and turned round to look down.

"I say, there's a dead rabbit down here."

A second boy joined him, peering. "It's not dead."

" 'Tis."

" 'Tisn't."

" 'Tis."

" 'Tisn't. All right, I'll show you."

The second put a hand on either side and lowered himself to the bottom. Stooping, he picked up the rabbit, which remained inert, laid it on the concrete verge and pulled himself up and out.

"I told you it was dead," said the first boy.

"I still don't believe it is. Wait, I'll get a blade of grass."

"Oh, leave it alone, both of you," cried an older girl, from beside the azaleas, "getting that nasty mess all over your hands! Leave it alone, Philip. Leave it where it is and

Hemmings'll take it away if you tell him. Coo-ee!" she called in a high-pitched voice. "We're com-ing!"

The boys, leaving the body of the rabbit on the concrete, followed her round a laurustinus, over some box bushes and out of sight. Two or three minutes later, Tindra and Nyreem came cautiously out from under the laurels and approached the edge of the pit.

"Sandwort!" said Tindra, sniffing at the body. "Sandwort! He isn't dead," she added to Nyreem. "He's breathing and his blood's moving. Lick his nostrils; lick his eyelids. That's right."

The two does persevered for several minutes. At length Sandwort's head moved slightly and his eyes opened. He tried to get on his feet but for some time could not do so.

"What happened? Where's the dog? Where's Foxglove?"

"Come back under the bushes, if you can," said Tindra. "The dog's gone, but you need to rest."

It was late in the evening when the two does at last reached the ridge of the Down, with Sandwort limping and stumbling beside them. The first rabbit they met was Fiver, who sniffed Sandwort over where he lay and went to tell Hazel.

"He'd better get some sleep," said Hazel grimly. "Take him to the nearest burrow," he added to Nyreem. "As for you," he went on, turning to Tindra, "you'd better stay with me and explain yourself. What were the two of you doing down there after I'd said no one was to go?"

Poor Tindra was so much overcome by the severity of the Chief Rabbit that she was able to come out with only an incoherent stammering of mixed-up excuses that amounted to no excuse at all. Hazel gave her a sound scolding, but this was modified by the indisputable fact (which she was too demoralized to put forward for herself) that if she and Nyreem had not done what they did, Sandwort would now be dead. It was left to Hazel finally to give her credit for that.

As for Sandwort, he was a changed rabbit. He never spoke of what he had undergone and became almost excessively respectful to his seniors. One evening, several weeks after the affair of the pit, Dandelion was acting as host to a hlessi who was staying a few days in the warren. At evening silflay he was pointing out one or two personalities, when the hlessi asked, "And who's that poor afflicted rabbit who sticks so close to his doe?"

"Where?" replied Dandelion, looking about them. "Oh, that's a rabbit called Sandwort, who's had an extraordinarily lucky escape. It happened like this . . ."

18

Stonecrop

Those stinks which the nostrils straight abhor are
not most pernicious, but such airs as have some similitude
with man's body, and so betray the spirits.

FRANCIS BACON, *Natural History*

Soon after sunrise on a perfect summer morning, Hazel
came out of his burrow, through the Honeycomb and into
the fresh air of the Down. Dusk and dawn are the activity
times for rabbits, and already a number were grazing in
twos and threes on the slope and out along the crest, paying
almost no attention even to one another as they foraged
through the short grass. It was a peaceful scene, and the
rabbits, knowing that they had no danger to fear, were ab-
sorbed in the enjoyment of feeding in the early sunshine.

Hazel watched them with satisfaction. Again and again,
since the previous spring, when Fiver's vision had brought
them up the steep hill to this high ground, he had acknowl-
edged the wisdom of choosing for a warren this lonely place
where rabbits could see all about them and consequently
had little to fear from their natural enemies. Scents, whether

the reassuringly accustomed or the disturbingly unusual, came to them on the prevailing west wind, while their great ears could readily detect the sounds made by an intruder, man or beast, who might approach over the chalk. It was a long time now, thought Hazel contentedly, since even one rabbit of his warren had fallen prey to an enemy. This was no easy hunting ground for the Thousand—fox, stoat, dog, marauding cat or any other enemy—while above all his rabbits were not persecuted by Man. Men, though their approach was the easiest to detect of all the elil, remained the most dreaded enemy, able with guns to kill from a distance and when on these hills almost as sharp-eyed as rabbits themselves. Frith be praised, thought Hazel, basking happily in the sun, we don't have to fear men in our daily lives; those sleek youngsters over there hardly know what a man is.

Suddenly, with a shock of surprise, he cast aside his tranquillity and became fully alert. From a short distance away, on the other side of the nearby trees, came the ugly sounds of rabbits fighting—yes, fighting among themselves, for among the high-pitched snarling and angry screeches he could hear nothing of any other animal. Nor could this be mating bucks fighting over a doe, for he could hear not two but three or four rabbits together.

In the normal way and apart from mating tussles, there was almost no fighting among the Watership Down rabbits. Since there were plenty of holes and plenty of grass, there was no occasion for it. Yet, as Hazel could now distinctly hear, this was a savage, bitter encounter, full of hatred and of desperation too. He turned and ran in the direction of the noise.

Coming out from among the trees, he saw at once what was going on. Three or four of his own rabbits, whom he recognized, were together setting upon a stranger. The stranger, not unnaturally, was getting the worst of it and was pinned to the ground. But insofar as Hazel could see, he was to all appearances a hulking great rabbit and had a good deal of fight left in him.

Hazel ran up to them and pulled two of the rabbits out of the scrimmage. The remaining two sat back on their haunches and looked at him.

"What's going on?" asked Hazel. "You, Peerton, and you, Woodruff—what are you trying to do?"

"We're going to kill him, Hazel-rah," panted the rabbit called Peerton, one of whose front paws looked badly bitten. "Let us alone. It won't take long."

"But what for? What's the matter?"

"Why, he doesn't just smell of men; he reeks of them," said Woodruff. "Can't you smell him, Hazel-rah? Wild rabbits always have to kill a rabbit who smells of men. You know that, surely?"

Hazel did know it; had always known it as an unalterable linchpin of rabbit lore. However, he had never before seen it being put into effect. These rabbits were putting it into effect by instinct, without stopping to ask questions.

Now, with the fighting having been broken off for the

moment, he certainly could smell the stranger. Involuntarily, the horrible stink made him tense with fear, so that he almost turned to run. With an effort, he pulled himself together. The four rabbits were watching his reaction closely.

"You can't say we're doing wrong, can you, Hazel-rah?" said Woodruff. "Just leave us to finish."

"No," said Hazel, with all the wavering determination he could muster. "I need to talk to him; to find out how he came to smell like this. There may be some danger threatening us all."

Meeting their eyes, he could see their antagonism. His authority was hanging in the balance. But to say more now would be to admit doubt, to blather. He waited silently.

Hazel's standing as Chief Rabbit was high. No one resented it, and he had no enemies. However, as he realized, it was touch and go now. At length, after a considerable pause, Peerton said, "Well, Hazel-rah, I hope you know what you're doing. Most of the warren aren't going to like this at all."

Still Hazel added nothing, only waiting for what he had said to prevail. Peerton looked round at his companions. Finally he said, "Everyone is going to hear of this," and slowly made off, the other three following him with no attempt to hide their feelings.

"Get up," said Hazel to the stranger. "You'd better come with me. In case you're wondering who I am, I'm the Chief Rabbit round here. You'll be safe with me."

The stranger, with some difficulty, scrambled to his

feet. There was an ugly, deep gash all across his back, and one of his ears was torn. Hazel, taking him in, realized that though young, he was of formidable size and build; almost as hefty as Bigwig.

"What's your name?" he asked.

"Stonecrop," replied the other.

"Well," said Hazel, "I want you to come with me to my burrow. I need to talk to you." And as Stonecrop hesitated: "Brace up. No one's going to hurt you."

They went together the short distance through the trees and down into the Honeycomb, where a little crowd of rabbits were loitering, chatting together and preparing to enjoy the fine day. As Stonecrop appeared, one and all shrank back in startled alarm and repulsion. In the enclosed Honeycomb, Stonecrop smelled still worse. Even those rabbits who had never actually smelled a man grew tense and horrified.

Hazel gazed round at them. "This is a rabbit I found outside just now. I know what you're all feeling, but I mean to talk to him, to find out something about him and how he came to smell like this."

"But great jumping horseflies, Hazel-rah!" cried Hawkbit. "What on earth—"

"Shut up!" replied Hazel sharply. "You all heard me. Let him alone. And Hyzenthlay, will you come with me to my burrow?"

Once again he had the strong impression that they were shocked and obeyed him only with difficulty. Every rabbit instinct, every pattern of rabbit behavior, was weighing against him. He forced himself to walk slowly across the Honeycomb, followed by Hyzenthlay and the badly frightened Stonecrop.

"Now take it easy," said Hazel, as soon as the three of them had reached his burrow. "Have a rest. Go to sleep if you like. How do you feel?"

"Could be worse," answered Stonecrop. "I'm ready to talk, if that's what you want."

"Well," said Hazel, "you obviously know, of course, that you smell very strongly of Man and that that's why all these rabbits are against you and feel they have to kill you. Hyzenthlay and I want to know how you've come to smell like this and whether we have anything to fear from the men you've been with."

For some little time, Stonecrop made no reply. At length he said, "I've never had anything to do with wild rabbits before."

"How's that come about, then?" said Hazel.

"I was born in a hutch," replied Stonecrop. "There were four of us in the litter, two does and two bucks—counting me, that is. As soon as our eyes were open and we had some fur, our mother told us how she'd been hit by a hrududu and knocked unconscious a good many days before we were born. The men in the hrududu, she said, had picked her up and taken her home with them. They'd expected her to die, but she didn't and they'd put her in this hutch, where she gave birth to us. There were two human children—girls—who used to give her food and water. She was a very big, strong doe, was our mother, and that's why she hadn't died when the hrududu hit her and why she didn't die in the hutch."

"What was her name?" asked Hyzenthlay.

"Thrennion," answered Stonecrop. "She told us that thrennions are pretty red berries that grow on bushes in winter, but of course I've never seen thrennion berries—not yet.

"Well, she recovered—or partly recovered, anyway— and was able to suckle us, so that we grew up. The human girls looked after us carefully, and as we got bigger they used to bring us dandelion leaves and chopped-up carrots— we learned those names from Mother. I was the biggest and strongest of us, and one of the human girls used to make a great fuss of me. She'd lift me out of the hutch and hold me to show to her friends. I think she hoped I'd grow up tame, but I didn't. I used to struggle, and I was always looking for a chance to get away; but she held me tightly. And anyway, before she took me out of the hutch, she used to shut all the doors and windows, so I thought there was no chance.

"I'm surprised we lived, for we were always fretting and pining. We were unhappy. Mother used to tell us stories about life in the wild and said that we must always be watching for any chance there might be to get away.

"Mother died. She just pined away, and after she'd gone we all began to feel even more desperate. I was the one with the best chance, because I was the girls' favorite and got lifted out of the hutch more than the others. And it was at one of these times, when she'd lifted me out, that I saw there was a hole in the wall—a hole at floor level. There was a man who used to scrub the floor—it was a smooth, hard floor—with a stiff broom, and he used to brush the dirty water out through that hole. I noticed carefully whereabouts it was.

"One day, not long ago, the two girls lifted me out to show a friend, another girl. And as near as I could make out, this other girl was begging to be allowed to hold me just for a few moments. She was older than the other two, and they didn't like to refuse her.

"The girl who was holding me was just passing me across to the bigger girl, when somehow or other she fumbled, and I felt that my back legs were free. I gave a tremendous backward kick and felt my claws tear this girl's bare arm all the way up. She screamed, and I just leaped and landed on the floor. The girls tried to grab me, but I scrambled away and ran like mad for the drain hole. I went straight through it and found myself in a yard.

"I had no idea which way to go. I simply ran. I was lucky. I got out of the yard and found myself in a field full of big animals. You call them cows, don't you? I ran across that and got into a lot of trees, and there I hid all night. No other animals troubled me, and now, of course, I know why.

"I wandered about, feeding and hiding, for quite a few days, and one night I met a hedgehog who didn't seem to mind the way I smelled. The hedgehog told me there were a lot of rabbits who lived up the hill. I stayed near him that night, and as soon as it began to get light I asked him the way. He said, 'Straight up the hill,' so up I went.

"I was just settling down for a rest in the grass at the top, when these rabbits—your rabbits, aren't they?—found me and sniffed me over. Then they all set upon me. I fought as hard as I could, but naturally the four of them got me down. They kept crying out, 'Kill him! Kill him!' and they *would* have killed me, sure enough, if you hadn't come and saved me.

"What's going to happen now? Are some other rabbits going to kill me? Are *you* going to kill me?"

"No," said Hazel. "Hyzenthlay and I will see to that. You're safe here. But for the moment you must stay in this burrow. Don't go out on any account. One of us will stay with you today."

"But whatever *are* we going to do with him?" asked Hyzenthlay. "You know the rabbit lore. The warren will never accept him."

"I know," replied Hazel, "but I'm not going to let him be killed—not if I can help it. Now I've heard his story, I'm entirely on his side."

"Then he'll have to stay here, in your burrow. He won't be safe anywhere else. And if we make him go away, he'll be quite helpless on his own against the elil."

"I know. I don't know what to do any more than you. But he'll have to eat, of course. I'll silflay with him myself after dark, when there's no one else about. You go back to the other rabbits now and try to find out whether any of them are ready to accept him. Talk to Bigwig. And Fiver too, if you can."

Hyzenthlay went. Hazel remained all day with Stonecrop, who seemed exhausted and slept most of the time. No other rabbits came to the burrow, until Hyzenthlay returned that evening.

"I'm afraid it's a bad lookout, Hazel-rah," she said. "Peerton and his friends have been telling everyone about Stonecrop and saying that not to kill him in accordance with custom would bring bad luck down on the warren. I haven't been able to find anyone, except Vilthuril and Thethuthinnang, who'd listen to me at all. Even Bigwig was very doubtful. He wouldn't say that you were right."

As soon as it was dark, the two of them took Stonecrop to silflay on the Down. He was not used to eating grass and in any case was too afraid and apprehensive to make much of a feed. In all manner of small respects and behavior he showed that he was different from normal wild rabbits and had not their ways. Hazel, noting this, felt close to despair on his behalf. He would probably never become a wild rabbit—not in months. However, he said nothing of this but only tried his best to encourage Stonecrop and make him feel that at any rate he had two friends. They got back to the burrow without meeting anyone.

Next morning, Fiver came to see them and in particular "to get an idea" of Stonecrop, as he put it. He said nothing about the smell but spent a long time talking to

Stonecrop, who evidently liked him and was drawn out to become more warm and responsive than he had been since coming to the warren.

"But what are we going to *do*, Fiver?" asked Hazel, as Fiver settled down beside Stonecrop and seemed to be making himself comfortable and ready to stay.

"I don't know," replied Fiver, "but just give me time, give me some time, Hazel. You're always so impatient."

"Well, you'd be impatient if you had to sit here and feel the whole warren seething at your back," said Hazel. "It's the first time I've ever felt that they weren't with me. I don't like it."

Fiver joined them that night on the silflay after dark, and had evidently gained Stonecrop's confidence to the extent of feeling able to correct and advise him about some of his ways which differed from those of wild rabbits.

"Cheer up," he said. "We've got two or three rabbits that we helped escape from a hutch last summer, and they've managed to live here all right. Of course, things were different then. We were desperate for does at any cost, and these rabbits didn't smell of men nearly so strongly as you. But you'll be all right, don't worry." And with that he went to sleep for the night.

On the following morning Bigwig unexpectedly came into the burrow, and at once recoiled from Stonecrop's smell.

"Frith on a hrududu! Hazel," he said, "I'd no idea it would be so strong. How can you stand it?"

"I hope you've come to give me some advice," said

Hazel, who felt really glad to see him. "I've missed you this last day or two."

"Well, I *will* give you some advice," answered Bigwig, "but you won't like it. Hazel-rah, the plain truth is that you can't hope to get this rabbit accepted in the warren. It's quite out of the question. Our rabbits simply won't have him, not for any inducement you can offer. Peerton and his friends have already seen to that. But even without Peerton, I don't believe they'd ever have accepted him. I mean, it's flying in the face of Nature, Hazel. I don't think El-ahrairah himself could get him accepted—and that's assuming he wanted to, which I don't believe he would. A rabbit who smells of Man has got to be killed, and that's been the way of it everywhere, time out of mind."

Hazel said nothing, and after a pause Bigwig went on: "But I'm afraid it's more serious than that, Hazel. The plain truth is that your position as Chief Rabbit is in real danger. Your authority's leaking away drop by drop as long as they don't see you, as long as they know you're holed up here with this accursed rabbit. Whatever you're up to, you've got to drop it, or else you'll be in bad trouble—worse than Fly-airth, I reckon. You simply can't afford to go on like this. For all our sakes, for the sake of the whole warren, give it up, now!"

Hazel still remained silent, and it was Fiver who spoke next.

"I'll tell you the thing to do, Hazel. Take Stonecrop to the new warren and ask Groundsel to have him. That's the answer, take it from me."

"But that's just plain stupid, Fiver," said Bigwig impatiently. "Groundsel's rabbits won't have him any more than our rabbits here."

"Yes, they will," answered Fiver calmly.

"Why should they? What makes you think so?"

"I don't know," said Fiver. "All I know for a certainty is that if Stonecrop's taken to Groundsel's warren he'll be all right. I haven't been able to see any more."

"Oh!" sneered Bigwig. "You've had a vision, I suppose, have you?"

Hazel spoke. "Wait a moment, Bigwig. Haven't you learned yet to trust Fiver? Wasn't he right about Cowslip's warren and the snares? About our raid on the farm? And about the idea that he put into my head of leading the dog onto the Efrafans? Vervain too—he defeated him without striking a blow. Fiver, you're sure about this, are you?"

"Yes, I'm sure enough that this is the thing to do, Hazel," answered Fiver. "I can't see how it'll turn out; something violent, it feels like. But it's what we must do, all right."

"That's good enough for me," said Hazel. "We'll start just before first light tomorrow—before any other rabbits are about. Bigwig, you'll come, won't you? I'd feel much better if I had you with us."

Bigwig paused for some little time. At length, rather hesitantly, he said, "All right, I will. And Frith help you, Fiver, if you're wrong."

"Hyzenthlay will stay here and tell them tomorrow

that we've gone," said Hazel. "I don't know when we'll be back, of course, but she'll be Chief Rabbit on her own until we do."

The three of them set off the next morning and by sunrise had already left Watership Down well behind them. Their progress soon grew slower, however, for Stonecrop, despite his size and strength, was quite unused to going any distance, and they were obliged to halt more and more frequently to let him rest. Bigwig was very patient and encouraged him in the most friendly way, but Hazel, who of course knew Bigwig through and through, could sense that he was not easy about the length of time that they were spending in the open, especially with a totally inexperienced rabbit who knew so little about ordinary rabbit ways and the innumerable small signals—mostly unconscious—with which rabbits communicate with one another on a journey.

As they were resting under a thick thornbush in the heat of the day, Stonecrop said to Bigwig, "I'm surprised that you both seem to be so much afraid of these elil, as you call them."

"Never met any, have you?" replied Bigwig.

"No, but if I do I won't run away; I'll fight. I'll fight any creature that tries to kill me."

"You've got a lot to learn," said Bigwig. "Some elil you can't fight; they're simply too much for any rabbit. Either you have to hide or else to run. I wouldn't like to see you throw your life away for nothing."

"Well, I don't like the idea of running away from an

enemy," said Stonecrop. "But of course I don't want to argue with you, when you're going to so much trouble to help me."

"You'll get on much better if you simply accept my advice," said Bigwig. "For the time being, anyway. But if you're rested enough now, we'd better be getting on. We've still got quite a long way to go."

During the afternoon they were only able to go even more slowly, and it was early evening before they drew near to Groundsel's warren. As they came within sight of it, both Hazel and Bigwig stopped sharply and sat up on their hind legs in alarm.

"There's something wrong," said Hazel.

"Yes, and badly wrong too!" exclaimed Bigwig. "What on earth can be happening? Look, it's as though they were all running for their lives."

As he spoke, they could see crowds of rabbits precipitately jumping from the holes in the bank and running away in all directions, plainly with no thought but escape. Hazel and Bigwig stared aghast.

"Look, there's Groundsel himself, running like the rest," said Hazel.

"I'll stop him," said Bigwig. "We've got to get to the bottom of this."

Running to their left, he got in front of Groundsel, who seemed unable even to see him but blundered straight into him and almost knocked him down. Bigwig jumped on him and pinned him to the ground.

"What is it, Groundsel?" asked Hazel. "Whatever's the matter?"

"Let me go, let me go!" squealed Groundsel. "Get off me, let me go!"

"Not until you've told us what the trouble is," said Hazel. "Have you all gone mad? Come on, talk to us."

"The weasels!" panted Groundsel. "Can't you see them? They're hunting through the warren. Let me go, damn you!"

Hazel and Bigwig stared down at the bank and its rabbit holes. There, sure enough, they could see the weasels—more than four in number—who were plainly hunting in a pack, from one end of the warren to the other. It was an appalling sight. They went racing from hole to hole and along the side of the bank, seemingly intensely excited. Like ants, they ran a little way very swiftly, then stopped and searched from side to side, before rejoining their companions to go on again in a straight line. The impression they gave was horribly systematic. Here and there one would thrust out its reddish head for a moment from a hole, then withdraw it and reappear from another. As they went they cried to one another in short, snappy sounds.

Hazel and Bigwig, affected by the panic no less than the other rabbits, were turning to run, when suddenly Stonecrop thrust them aside.

"I'm not afraid!" he cried. "I'm not afraid of those dirty little beasts, those elil or whatever you call them. Come on, follow me!"

With that he went forward, straight for the bank.

"Stonecrop, come back!" cried Bigwig. "Come back—they'll kill you!"

"I'll be damned if they will," answered Stonecrop, and broke into a run which took him into the very midst of the weasels on the bank.

Hazel saw them turn to pull him down. But what was this? The two nearest to him suddenly recoiled, sniffing, and squeaking to the others in fear. Then all of them took up the squeaking in their nasty, shrill little voices: "Man! Man! Run! Man!"

All together they tumbled down the bank, picked themselves up at the foot and fled in a terrified gaggle into the copse beyond.

"You see?" said Stonecrop, as Hazel and Bigwig, still trembling, rejoined him at the foot of the bank. "Horrible little creatures! I'd soon have put paid to a few of them if they hadn't all run away."

Slowly, and one by one, the other rabbits returned, staring at Stonecrop as though at some supernatural being. Finally Groundsel returned, together with three or four of his Owsla, all of whom were badly shaken.

"I *saw* you!" said one of them to Stonecrop. "I *saw* you with my own eyes, chasing the weasels away! I still can't believe what I saw!"

"Nothing to it," replied Stonecrop. "Anyone could have done it. It's just a matter of standing up to them, that's all."

"No," said Hazel, giving Groundsel the prescribed

salute of one Chief Rabbit to another, "not quite all. It strikes me we turned up just in time. Groundsel-rah, may I explain who this rabbit is and how Bigwig and I come to be here with him?"

By this time a few more of the Owsla had come back, and Hazel, sitting down among them, told them everything about Stonecrop, about the trouble at Watership Down and about Fiver's advice that they should bring him here and ask Groundsel to let him join.

"Let him join?" said Groundsel, when Hazel had finished. "Let you join?" he said, turning to Stonecrop. "You've saved the whole warren! You can stay for many, many years if you like! You can have your own personal burrow and choose any doe you fancy! And in return, all I ask is that you walk slowly round all the runs in the warren every morning and evening, to see they smell right."

Hazel and Bigwig stayed a few days, as Groundsel's guests. The weather remained perfect, and they had the satisfaction of seeing Stonecrop not only accepted but treated almost as a celebrity by the other rabbits.

"So Fiver was right," said Bigwig one evening, as they were at silflay under a crimson sky.

"He's always right," replied Hazel. "It's just as well for us, isn't it?"

19

Campion

Though it appear a little out of fashion,
There is much care and valour in this Welshman.

WILLIAM SHAKESPEARE, *Henry V*

The weather remained fine, and Groundsel's rabbits, having more or less got over the bad shock of the weasels' attack, made good progress with their warren, which came to be known by the name of Vleflain. A good number, both from Watership and from Efrafa, were pregnant does, whose natural instinct is to dig burrows. The males busied themselves chiefly with internal runs linking together the various parts of the warren. Any human being who has gone ferreting in an old warren will know to what almost incredible distances internal runs can extend. However, the founders of Vleflain were not disturbed by ferrets or any other mustelidae, and it looked as though Groundsel's anxiety about nearby stoats had been unjustified.

Hazel did not trouble himself to make another journey to Vleflain but rested content with now-and-then reports from Kehaar that all was going well. He had never himself met Avens, the leader of the Efrafan party, but saw no reason to doubt Groundsel's opinion that he was well up to the job.

Hazel's veterans, who felt it a great improvement that numbers in the Watership warren had been reduced to a comfortable level, shared his view. "It's a case of 'no news is good news,' Hazel-rah," said Bigwig. "If they'd met with any kind of danger or trouble, they'd have let us know quick enough. Two or three more of our rabbits here have asked me whether they can go and join them. I ought really to have sent and asked Groundsel first, but I was sure it would be all right, and I just told them to ask Kehaar to show them the way."

Summer was well advanced when, one fine evening, with everyone at silflay, no less a rabbit than Buckthorn turned up, with a message from Groundsel begging Hazel to come and advise him as soon as he could.

"Why? Is there trouble?" asked Hazel.

"Well, not exactly trouble," replied Buckthorn. "At least, you could call it trouble, in a manner of speaking. We're very worried about it, Hazel-rah. But I promised Groundsel that I'd leave it to him to tell you about it when you came. He said that if you needed persuading, I could tell you that it involved Efrafa."

"Efrafa? Oh, confound it all!" said Hazel. "I thought we'd settled all that long ago. Well, I suppose Fiver and I had better go tomorrow, if the weather stays fine. If you don't fancy making the journey back so soon, why don't you stay in my burrow for a few days, see some old friends, and go back when you're ready? By the way," he added, "why have I got to go down there? Why can't Groundsel come up here, if he wants to see me?"

"Well, he's arranging a meeting," replied Buckthorn, "and I rather think Captain Campion's coming."

"Campion? Oh, great Frith, it must be something really awkward," said Hazel. "Wherever *he* is, there's trouble, or there always used to be. I've learned that, all right."

He and Fiver set out for Vleflain the following morning, with protection, from time to time, from Kehaar. They arrived late in the afternoon and found Groundsel almost too effusively glad to welcome them. "Oh, we'll be all right now you two are here," he said. "Come and have a good rest in the sun and tell me all about friends back at home. How's that wretched Sandwort getting on? Why don't you send him along to us? The change'd do him good."

"He'd never get here in his present state," said Fiver. "It'll be quite a long time before he's recovered. A lot of rabbits wouldn't have survived what he went through."

"Let's have a run round your warren," said Hazel. "I'd like to see what you've all made of it. You're all comfortable, I hope?"

"Oh, very," replied Groundsel. "Plenty of room here, you know, and that makes a lot of difference. I've even taken one or two more from Efrafa—friends I knew last year, when I was an Efrafan myself. As you'd expect, they say it's much better there without Woundwort."

Hazel and Fiver slept with Groundsel in his burrow and were woken early next morning by a young rabbit bringing a message. "Captain Campion's here, Groundsel-rah," he said, "and he says he's ready to talk whenever you like."

"Where'd you get that 'Captain' from?" snapped Groundsel. "He's 'Campion-rah' to you, don't you know that?"

"I'm sorry, sir," said the youngster. "It's just that everybody speaks of him as 'Captain,' and I've got into the way of it."

They went out into a beautifully fresh, clear morning and found Campion sitting in the sun at the foot of the bank. He and Hazel greeted each other with embarrassment and a certain reserve. On the last occasion when they had been together, that terrible evening on Watership Down, Campion had asked Woundwort whether he should kill Hazel. Neither had forgotten that, though both were anxious that no mention of it should be made now. As Strawberry came up to join them, Hazel was able to cover the awkward moment by greeting him as an old friend and follower and by asking him how he liked life in the new warren. Strawberry replied for the most part with praise of his rabbits, who, he said, had worked hard and settled in very well, those from both Watership and Efrafa.

"Campion," began Groundsel, "although you've been Chief Rabbit of Efrafa for a long time now—ever since the disappearance of Woundwort last summer, in fact—you've been having a lot to do with this warren of mine, haven't you? You've been here a good deal."

"Yes, I have," answered Campion.

"He's too distinguished and proud to make any excuses or hold anything back," thought Hazel. "Whatever this is all about, at least we shan't have to squeeze information out of him or tell him he's lying."

"Anyone who wants to come," went on Campion, "I take them out on Wide Patrol."

"Why don't you stick to taking out your own Efrafans?"

"Because they won't come," replied Campion without hesitation. "Not one of them."

"Why not, do you know?"

"Because they associate Wide Patrols with Woundwort," said Campion. "They don't want anything that they think has to do with Woundwort."

"Well, haven't Wide Patrols got a lot to do with Woundwort? Isn't that quite right?"

"Certainly," said Campion, and waited silently for Groundsel to go on.

"He invented them, didn't he?"

"Yes."

"Yet you come here and fill my rabbits up with Woundwort's ideas?"

"No, I don't. I simply take out on Wide Patrol any rabbits who want to come."

"And that's all? You don't tell them about Woundwort and what he did?"

"No. I never mention Woundwort."

"And you aren't planning to influence enough rabbits to fight for you so that you can take over this warren?"

"Certainly not."

"Well, I think you are."

"None of the rabbits I've taken out on Patrol can have told you that."

"Why not?"

"Because I always assure them that I've got no such plans. I haven't the least wish to take over Vleflain."

"Then why come here and persuade my rabbits to go out on Wide Patrols with you?"

"I don't persuade them. They're eager to come."

"Because of the influence of your personality. They want to feel that you're their friend."

Campion made no reply.

"Isn't that so?"

"Possibly."

"You're a distinguished rabbit. You were Woundwort's best officer. You led the assault at Nutley Copse. You did everything you could to help him take the Efrafans to destroy Hazel's warren, and you brought the survivors back to Efrafa when no one else could have done it. Do you really think that my rabbits aren't going to admire you and want to be like you?"

"They may. But as I've said, all I do is take out on Wide Patrol any rabbits who want to come."

"What for?"

"For my enjoyment and their good."

"And that's all?"

"Yes."

There was a pause. A young rabbit came up to speak to Groundsel, who dismissed him with a curt "Not now. Not now." It was Fiver who spoke next.

"You say for your 'enjoyment and their good.' Could you perhaps tell us a little more about that? What do you enjoy and what do you think does them good?"

Campion remained silent for some little time, as though meditating on his reply. When next he began to speak, it was in a relaxed, almost gentle tone, very different from his hitherto sharp, brief replies.

"To have grown up in Efrafa, to have begun by admiring Woundwort although far below his notice; then to have become an officer and after a time to realize that you were one of the few rabbits that he respected and relied upon to carry out what he wanted, even though he wasn't there himself—these are the experiences which have made me what I am, good or bad. They've made me self-reliant, able to think for myself; to think for Woundwort and act for him when he wasn't there to tell me what to do—all this has been my entire life. And now that he's gone, no one can expect me to forget his influence in a matter of months. Of course, I've realized now all he did, all he thought, that was wrong. I needn't tell it to you now."

He paused, but no one spoke, and after a little he continued.

"Bringing those survivors back, alone, from Watership to Efrafa last summer—that was the hardest thing I've ever had to do, and do without the General. It called on every particle of strength and self-reliance I'd got; it nearly killed me; and when we'd got back and I'd recovered, why wouldn't I feel proud of what I'd done? I knew then what I was capable of.

"But I didn't show it. I was half expecting to be killed by the rabbits who'd hated Woundwort and had only been held back by Vervain and by Woundwort's own authority.

"But they didn't kill me. They made me Chief Rabbit. They needed me to think for them and act for them; to dismantle Woundwort bit by bit and persuade them to keep the parts that made sense.

"There was one part that to me made more sense than all the rest put together, and that was the Wide Patrols. Woundwort always said, again and again, that rabbits didn't have to run away or to hide in holes. They could beat the elil if only they had the determination and self-confidence to do it. And to get that, they had to learn how to be wary, self-reliant, tenacious and brave. And that they learned through the Wide Patrols.

"To be taking out a Wide Patrol on a fine morning—there's nothing more wonderful in the world. To know that they trust you and want to come with you; to know there'll be danger and not to care, and to make them feel like that too. And then if danger suddenly becomes a reality, to stand up to it and either beat it or escape by using your wits. And to see your rabbits, the three or four with you on the Patrol, improving all the time, until they become fit to lead a Patrol themselves—that's all very enjoyable, I assure you. Wide Patrols make cunning trackers, swift runners and brave fighters. You know this, Groundsel. You've been an Efrafan officer and must have been on quite a few Patrols yourself."

As he paused and looked about him at his questioners, Hazel asked, "But weren't rabbits killed on these Patrols?"

"No more than we could afford to lose," answered Campion. "When I'd got Efrafa back to something like normal, last autumn, I tried to get the Wide Patrols started again, but not a rabbit would come. They said they'd had enough of what they called 'Woundwort's fancy ways.' So I had to drop it. To go on pressing them would probably have been the right way to get myself killed.

"But I still longed to take out a Wide Patrol myself. I wanted it for my own enjoyment and nothing more. But you can't do a Wide Patrol by yourself. You'd know if you'd ever tried. The mutual reliance and the comradeship aren't there.

"So I came up here to see if things were any different at Vleflain. They were. I didn't have to coax or wheedle anyone. Right from the start I had the material for three or four Patrols and more. And this is what I mean by saying it's for my enjoyment and their good. The rabbits I've taken out are far, far better for it."

"But isn't it true," persisted Hazel, "that quite a lot of rabbits have been killed or lost on these Patrols of yours?"

"I wouldn't say a lot," said Campion. "I'd say a few. And that's the price that has to be paid, of course, for all that's gained."

"Why didn't you come and speak to me first?" said Groundsel. "I'm the Chief Rabbit here, in case it's happened to escape your notice."

"Don't you talk like that to me," flashed Campion. "I remember when you were a nobody. And if you want the real answer, it's because I didn't want to ask any favors from a junior Efrafan officer."

"But we're not in Efrafa now," said Groundsel. "We're in Vleflain and I'm the Chief Rabbit."

Before the bristling Campion could reply, Fiver spoke again.

"Let's break off for a bit now, shall we? I'd like to have a go at your dandelions, Groundsel. They smell first-rate, better than anything we've got up on the Down. Dandelions don't seem to favor the downs, somehow."

Taking Hazel with him, he moved off a little way along the bank, where the two remained in earnest talk for quite some time. When they had rejoined the others, Hazel at once said, "Campion-rah, how would you like to come and stay in our warren for a bit? You could do all the patrolling you liked, and we've got plenty of young rabbits who would jump at the chance of going out with you. I'm sure they'd all be much the better for it, once you'd settled in and got started."

Both Groundsel and Campion seemed taken aback.

Neither made any reply, and Hazel went on: "I know one rabbit who'd be more than pleased to see you, and that's Bigwig. He's often spoken of you in the most admiring terms and wanted to know you better."

It was plain that Campion was not averse to the idea. As he remained silent, Fiver put in, "I'm sure they could find someone to look after Efrafa for a little while. Nothing like as good as you, of course, but if they did get into any sort of trouble, you could easily be back there in a day and a half. Kehaar could let you know at once if you were needed."

"Very well," replied Campion at last. "I shall be glad to come for a time. I should certainly like to meet Bigwig again—as a friend this time. But I think a lot of your younger rabbits are going to miss me, Groundsel. That's the plain truth."

"You could always lead one of your Wide Patrols down here and see them again," said Groundsel, half seriously. "It's not really all that far."

When Campion broke the news to his friends and admirers in Vleflain, there was much disappointment. Two of these, a pair named Loosestrife and Knapweed, begged Hazel to let them come too, and Groundsel made no objection.

They started next day and reached Watership without any trouble from elil. Hyzenthlay, although certainly taken by surprise, welcomed Campion and his followers, while Hazel allotted them a burrow for themselves. (It had been Flyairth's.)

Campion had the sense to begin in a small way, with

short, easy Patrols, which Bluebell called "there and back." One of his first and keenest recruits was Sandwort, although Campion, when he had sized him up, said that he ought to restrict himself to undemanding work—for the time being at least. Bigwig, having joined in a long and exhausting Patrol into the country west of Beacon Hill, told Hazel and Fiver that Campion's leadership was impressive and, he thought, better than his own.

"Thank goodness they've taken to each other," said Fiver. "I was afraid they might not."

The first casualty occurred round about midsummer, when a doe named Lemista, having damaged her front paw, fell victim to a dog, which killed her before Campion could drive it off. Hazel was upset, but Bigwig, like Campion, regarded it as "the price to be paid." "Wherever that rabbit was doing his work, Hazel-rah," he said, "—and he does it very well—there'd be bound to be occasional casualties; and our rabbits are no different from any other rabbits."

"Oh, yes, they are," answered Hazel. "They're different when you know them personally." But he did nothing to check or change what Campion was doing; there was no general demand that he should do so. The younger rabbits admired Campion. He made no enemies. They considered him a unique asset to the warren. You were not really respected until you had done a few Patrols.

In the event, he stayed on until he became an accepted institution: a gaunt, gray rabbit somewhat given to entrusting Patrol leadership to his best and most reliable followers, although what every learner wanted was to be taught by him. "Anyone can do it once they've learned how," he used to say. "A lot of them can do it better than me." But it was not true, and his standards remained as exacting as ever.

For one quality in particular they all thought the world of him: he never carped. He never said the equivalent of "These young rabbits nowadays, they're not like we used to be." On the contrary, he was warm and full of encouraging praise for his youngsters. "But don't start thinking you're good," he would add. "It's not me, it's the elil who'll show you whether you're any good when you come across them. And you can't afford to be wrong. You realize that, don't you?"

He died on a Patrol, as he would have wished. One showery afternoon in April, out beyond Kingsclere, a Patrol he was leading encountered two wandering cats at close quarters. All five rabbits stood their ground, and there was a sharp tussle before the cats were glad enough to make their escape. Campion, however, was mortally wounded and died where he had fallen.

He, too, like Woundwort, in time became a legend. On dark, rainy evenings, if a benighted Patrol became lost and uncertain, a spirit of confidence would enter the leader's heart and guide them home. This they knew to be Captain Campion, onetime hero of Efrafa, but no less a hero to the rabbits of Watership Down.

Lapine Glossary

Efrafa	The name of the warren founded by General Woundwort.
El-ahrairah	The rabbit folk hero. The name (Elil-hrair-rah) means "Enemies-Thousand-Prince" = the Prince with a Thousand Enemies.
Elil	Enemies (of rabbits).
Embleer	Stinking, e.g., the smell of a fox.
Flay	Food, e.g., grass or other green fodder.
Flayrah	Unusually good food, e.g., lettuce.
Frith	The sun, personified as a god by rabbits. Frithrah! = the lord Sun—used as an exclamation.
Fu Inlé	After moonrise.
Hlessi	A rabbit living aboveground, without a regular hole or warren. A wandering rabbit, living in the open. (Plural, hlessil.)
Hrair	A great many; an uncountable number; any number over four. U Hrair = The Thousand (enemies).
Hrairoo	"Little Thousand." The name of Fiver in Lapine.

Hraka	Droppings, excreta.
Hrududu	A tractor, car or any motor vehicle. (Plural, hrududil.)
Hyzenthlay	Literally, "Shine-Dew-Fur" = Fur shining like dew. The name of a doe.
Inlé	Literally, the moon; also, moonrise. But a second meaning carries the idea of darkness, fear and death.
Lendri	A badger.
Narn	Nice, pleasant (to eat).
Ni-Frith	Noon.
Owsla	The strongest rabbits in a warren; the ruling clique.
Rah	A prince, leader or Chief Rabbit. Usually used as a suffix. E.g., Hazel-rah = Lord Hazel.
Roo	Used as a suffix to denote a diminutive. E.g., Hrairoo.
Sayn	Groundsel.
Silf	Outside, that is, not underground.
Silflay	To go aboveground to feed. Literally, to feed outside. Also used as a noun.
Tharn	Stupefied, distraught, hypnotized with fear. But can also, in certain contexts, mean "looking foolish," or "heartbroken" or "forlorn."
Thethuthinnang	"Movement of Leaves." The name of a doe.

Thlay	Fur.
Thlayli	"Furhead." Bigwig's name in Lapine.
Threar	A rowan tree, or mountain ash.
Thrennion	Berries of a rowan tree.
Vair	To excrete, pass droppings.
Yona	A hedgehog. (Plural, yonil.)
Zorn	Destroyed, murdered. Denotes a catastrophe.